ry

Shadows on the Train

Melanie Jackson

ORCA BOOK PUBLISHERS

Library and Archives Canada Cataloguing in Publication

Jackson, Melanie, 1956-
Shadows on the train / written by Melanie Jackson.

(A Dinah Galloway mystery)
ISBN 978-1-55143-660-9

I. Title. II. Series: Jackson, Melanie 1956- . Dinah Galloway mystery.

PS8569.A265S53 2007   jC813'.6   C2006-906704-X

First published in the United States, 2007
Library of Congress Control Number: 2006939250

Summary: Dinah is trapped on a cross-country train—in more danger than ever.

Orca Book Publishers gratefully acknowledges the support for its publishing
programs provided by the following agencies: the Government of Canada
through the Book Publishing Industry Development Program and the Canada
Council for the Arts, and the Province of British Columbia through the BC Arts
Council and the Book Publishing Tax Credit.

Cover design by Lynn O'Rourke and John van der Woude
Train photo credit: Michael Tension

Orca Book Publishers
PO Box 5626, Stn. B
Victoria, BC Canada
V8R 6S4

Orca Book Publishers
PO Box 468
Custer, WA USA
98240-0468

www.orcabook.com
Printed and bound in Canada.

010 09 08 07 • 4 3 2 1

I ran to the door, even though I wasn't supposed to answer it on my own. At five, I'd already established a firm pattern of not following instructions. I squinted at the man on the front step.

"Somethin' wrong with your eyes, kid?" he asked me and gave the laugh-cough of a heavy smoker.

"I might have to get glasses," I informed him. (I did, soon after.) "But I'd need a pair of binoculars to see where your hairline begins."

I was getting lots of talks from Mother and Dad about making personal remarks to people. How these remarks, even if true, can hurt people's feelings. However, the man just laugh-coughed at me. He wasn't the uptight type. "Nuthin' wrong with your voice, though, kid. Sure packs a wallop. Plannin' to sing at Carnegie Hall one day?"

He chuckle-coughed, but I didn't find it funny. I took my singing seriously. My Dad encouraged me to. Besides, I found singing—well, such a *relief*. Through my voice I could use up my energy, which I had a lot of.

"Yes, I *am* planning to sing at Crumbly Hall," I said boldly, despite not having heard of the place. I could never resist a challenge. Besides, to me a "hall" was our church hall at St. Cecilia's, a basement where teas and St. Valentine's dinners were held. "I might just go there this week."

That really set him off. He laugh-coughed so hard he had to back up to our flowerbed and spit into the pink cabbage roses.

Chapter One

The Knave of Hearts

I thought I'd met Ardle McBean for the one and only time seven years ago, just before my dad got drunk, crashed his car into a tree and died. Ardle was grizzled, with wispy, pale brown hair almost the color of his scalp. You had to squint to see his hair, as if it were one of those optical illusion tests. Which made Ardle himself seem not quite real, like a dream. Or maybe a nightmare.

When the doorbell rang, I was belting out a kids' song called "Black Socks"—

Black socks, they never get dirty,
The longer you wear them
The blacker they get.
Someday I think I will wash them,
But something keeps telling me
Don't do it yet,
Not yet, not yet.

Preface

Old sins cast long shadows
—ENGLISH PROVERB

Take it from me, Dinah Galloway. You think the past is gone. It isn't. It comes back.

Like the broccoli you stashed under your bed three weeks ago that starts to smell up your room. Or the annoying piano practice tunes from the Edna May Oliver exercise book that soft-shoe into your brain.

Or the jailbird friend of your late dad.

Thank you to the tracks of my life: Bart and Sarah-Nelle
Jackson. What a wonderful journey you give me.

MJ

And to Dinah's friends:
Visit Dinah on her blog
—never a blah-g, she promises—
www.dinahgalloway.blogspot.com

"That oughtta cut down on this week's watering," I commented.

It was a hot, hot summer, the kind where you can see the heat wavering in the still air. As if the world is holding its breath for something to happen. This man was the type to make things happen, I thought. Good or bad things, I wasn't sure.

It was then that Dad's hand landed on my shoulder and whisked me behind him. "Ardle McBean," he said, "I thought I'd talked you into turning yourself in."

I peeked round Dad's legs at Ardle. "Turning yourself into what?" I inquired with great interest. I was heavily into fairy tales at that point.

Ardle, whose thin face had grown glum at Dad's remark, cheered up again. He lit a cigarette, took a deep drag on it and laugh-coughed all the time he was exhaling. "To the cops, kid. I pulled a break-and-enter last week and was dumb enough to leave my fingerprints all over the place. Old McBean is slippin'!

"But, see," he bent down confidingly, "there's somethin' your dad's keeping for me. In an envelope, like. I just need to know it's safe."

Dad demanded, "You know the dangers of secondhand smoke to a kid?" He pushed me behind him again; I popped right out, like a jack-in-the-box.

Ardle laugh-coughed. "Okay, I'll git. I just wanted to make sure the king was okay, that's all. Guess you don't want to talk about the king in front o' the kid, though."

He gestured at me with his cigarette, scattering ashes over the porch Mother had just swept. "That sure is some songbird you got there, Mike. She makes 'Black Socks' sound like a Broadway show."

Dad grinned at me. "How do the lyrics to that go?" he teased and crooned:

Dinah's socks,
That she never washes,
You'd hardly notice
One from the next.

"No, no!" I exclaimed, jumping up and down. "Not like *that*, Dad."

But Dad was narrowing his eyes at Ardle. "The king is safe, okay? Hidden, so no one will find him. We clear on that?"

"Yeah, we're clear," Ardle said.

"We can discuss it more at the—" Dad glanced down at me and amended, "downtown."

At the *bar*, I thought wisely. That was the place Mother and Dad had shouting matches about, late at night. I'd wake up and hear them. I wasn't exactly clear on the bar concept, except that when Dad came home his words fell all over each other, and his breath smelled like cleaning disinfectant. Once he'd come into my room and cried.

It sure was more fun when he *didn't* go to this bar place. He and Mother would laugh a lot. He told the funniest stories. My older sister Madge, who worshipped him, would sit and glow. When sober, Dad was magnetic.

And he'd play our ancient piano while I sang.

We'd bought the piano from our church for fifty bucks. Dad had tuned it, which Father Rourke called a miracle because, A, the piano was considered junk and, B, Dad had tuned a guitar before, but never a piano.

Dad had so many talents. He just never seemed to organize them very well.

Anyhow, Ardle McBean shuffled his grizzled gaze from Dad to me. "Okay, Mike. I just wanted to make sure about the king. Y'know, in case I get put away for a while."

"What king?" I asked. I ransacked my brain. "The King of Hearts?"

I began jumping up and down again. "'The King of Hearts called for the tarts and beat the Knave full sore.'" Then I repeated the line, only louder, with bigger jumps. "'...AND BEAT THE KNAVE FULL SORE!'"

Instead of looking irritated, as most adults would've, Ardle regarded me with bemusement. "And folks say there's an energy crisis," he cracked. I grinned at him.

Dad didn't. "ARDLE."

Ardle held up hands with fingertips yellow-stained from nicotine. "I'm goin', I'm goin'."

Backing away, Ardle tripped against the bicycle-plus-training-wheels I'd left to one side of the front path. He spun in a maelstrom of flailing skinny legs and arms before crash-landing in Mother's violets. "Whoa, Nellie," he exclaimed, and his laugh-cough hacked out merrily.

Ardle sure was a good sport, I marveled. Last week

a similar mishap had occurred to a door-to-door entertainment-book salesman. *He'd* threatened to sue.

As Ardle laugh-coughed his way down the long Grandview neighborhood hill, I tugged at Dad's hand. And re-tugged. He seemed kind of distracted.

"Is Ardle the Knave of Hearts?" I demanded. I still had the nursery rhyme going through my head.

I was also trying to joke Dad out of his faraway thoughts. Usually I could do this. But this time he looked down and gave me a sad smile.

"I guess if anyone's the Knave of Hearts around here, I am," Dad said.

That didn't make sense to me, not then.

But I was right about that hot, still summer. Something was waiting to happen, and it did. Within three weeks, Dad was dead.

After that I forgot all about Ardle McBean, except for a comment I overheard at Dad's funeral. One of Dad's friends was talking to someone else: "Ardle? Oh, he's in the slammer again. Once a thief, always a thief. Turned himself in, though, I hear, thanks to Mike."

I didn't forget about Dad's Knave of Hearts remark, though. It bothered me for a long time. Then, one day this past year, I was in a sound studio, recording a new jingle for Sol's Salami on West Fourth. The sound people were all ready. I opened my mouth to belt my heart out, even if the song *was* about extra-garlic salami.

My dad told me to put my heart into my singing, so I always do.

And all at once, thinking about belting my heart out, I got it. I understood what Dad had meant. *He* was the Knave of Hearts; that's what he'd been saying. The Knave, the unreliable one, the scoundrel.

Dad must've sensed that, with his drinking, he'd one day disappear and take our hearts with him.

And he did.

Chapter Two
A Discordant Piano Lesson

I thumped the piano keys, PING, PANG, *PONNGG*!! higher and higher up the scale. I liked making the high notes sound like screams.

For good measure, even though high notes weren't in the Edna May Oliver exercise book propped in front of me, I struck them again. *PONNGG*!! Out the living room window the notes charged, hurtling down our East Vancouver street to Commercial Drive.

Colorful, with lots of delis and galleries, the Drive is a tourist attraction. Well, it was my civic duty to welcome visitors with a flourish, I decided. I thumped the keys some more.

My white and pumpkin-pie-colored cat, Wilfred, accompanied me with my playing. To the beat of my *PONNGG*s, Wilfred clawed fresh grooves in our old plush sofa. "He and I oughtta form a duet!" I shouted over the music at Mrs. Chewbley.

Mrs. Chewbley had such an odd expression on her face. She'd scrunched her features right up as if she were in pain. Oh well, I thought. That must be how piano teachers smile with delight. Soon Mrs. Chewbley would be telling everyone about her gifted student, twelve-year-old Dinah Galloway, the powerhouse pianist.

Shoving my glasses up my freckled nose, I splayed my fingers again for a fresh attack on the high-note keys.

"AAAGGGHHH..."

Whoa. That was pretty impressive—considering I hadn't actually lowered my fingers to the keys this time.

Hey, that was Mrs. Chewbley screaming. I followed her bulging-eyed gaze out the open living room window.

A green face with pointed teeth covered in blood was gaping in at us from among the hydrangeas.

"Oh hi, Pantelli," I greeted my buddy.

Pantelli Audia pulled the mask from his face and rested it on his untidy black curls. "Hi, Di. Sorry, Mrs. Chewbley. I just wanted to find out if Dinah had packed yet. For our train trip back east," he added as Mrs. Chewbley continued to tremble from the shock.

Hairpins were dripping from the piano teacher's untidy hairdo; her gray bird's nest bun was collapsing. With an effort, she managed a weak smile at Pantelli. He was her star pupil, up to grade eight in piano. His family's mantelpiece was crammed with all the gleaming trophies he'd won.

Mrs. Chewbley assured him, "I know that you, Dinah, and Talbot St. John will be performing together on *Tomorrow's Cool Talent*, that Toronto TV show. I'll be watching proudly, I promise you."

Talbot St. John, who lived down the street, rounded out our three-person ensemble by playing guitar. Talbot was the studious, conscientious type adults adored. He had solemn brown eyes and a long forelock of dark hair that some girls found attractive—okay, I did too, though only very mildly.

The chance to appear on *Tomorrow's Cool Talent* had come up a few weeks earlier, when the show's host had overheard us. That is, overheard Pantelli on piano, Talbot on guitar, and me on—well, on pipes, I guess you'd say. We had just solved a mystery in North Vancouver involving spotted owls and hang gliders. My sister Madge and I had been house-sitting in a posh neighborhood.

But I Di-gress.

Anyhow, we would be going to Toronto by train because Pantelli threw up on planes. He didn't make any promises about not barfing on the train, but said it was less likely. Still, Talbot was firm about not taking a sleeping berth below Pantelli.

Mr. Wellman, my agent, would be coming with us, and so would Madge. Her fiancé, Jack French, planned to fly to Toronto and meet us for a mini-holiday.

Jack's summer job was coordinating a wildlife preservation group, which led to a lot of tiresome jokes about how he'd also have to look out for the wildlife, i.e., yours truly, back east. Unfunny. Like I always say, these older folk should leave the jokes to me.

"I'm particularly looking forward to hearing you, Pantelli. Your playing is divine," Mrs. Chewbley was busy oozing. "So subtle..." She gave me a despairing glance.

I would've been insulted, except that Mrs. Chewbley, who was plump and jolly, had a mega sweet tooth just like me. Every time she came over, she unwrapped a box of mint creams or strawberry truffles or something equally yummy and non-nourishing. So I wasn't rude to her, and I never put glue on her side of the piano bench or anything like that.

Not that I would, at the lofty age of twelve and two-thirds, but...you know. Thoughts do flit across one's mind.

"We'll chat later," Mrs. Chewbley said fondly to Pantelli. "For now, Dinah has her lesson. She needs to finish her—er, playing."

"BOO-WAAA-HA-HA" was Pantelli's evil response. He slipped the mask back on and sank slowly into the hydrangeas. This would have had the sinister effect he no doubt intended, except for the pained screech that followed—"*Yeeow*! A wasp!"

"Maybe we should shut the window," Mrs. Chewbley suggested.

"To prevent the wasp from flying in?"

"To prevent the neighbors from having to hear you play."

I began a menacing scowl in slow motion. This was my new technique, based on the theory that a slo-mo scowl is much more frightening than a quick one. I got the idea from this story our teacher read aloud last year, "The Pit and the Pendulum," by Edgar Allan Poe. Instead of a quick death, the prisoner is sentenced to watch a knife-sharp pendulum swing down toward him. Slowly...slowly...

Sorry, I got a bit carried away there. That story's such *fun*. Anyhow, I was just turning my mouth down at both ends to match my scrunched-up eyes when Mrs. Chewbley gave *another* scream.

As before, she was gaping out the window. This time she also jumped, so the box of strawberry truffles that we'd only half polished off tumbled from her lap. Wilfred left the side of the sofa, where he'd been waiting for me to start playing again, to trot over and sniff the scattered truffles.

"Pantelli, give it a break, will you?" I demanded.

Then I heard it—the echo of the summer seven years ago when I lost my Dad.

A laugh-cough.

I unscrunched my eyes, and there he was, grinning at us across the windowsill. Ardle McBean. More lined than I remembered, and that optical-illusion hairline had retreated. What hair he had hung in long straggles, not unlike the wisps of smoke twisting from the cigarette he held.

Mrs. Chewbley let loose another scream.

"Obviously an anti-smoker," Ardle joked and cackled.

I was in rerun land. I was having a triple-decker sensation that went like this: Ardle was here, therefore I must be five again, and therefore Dad would appear with dadly indignation and be all angry and protective.

Fast forward, Dinah. Not Dad's hand on my shoulder, but the icy, unsympathetic hand of reality. I was on my own, Dadless. Now and lifelong.

"Hey," said Ardle, leaning over the sill. "You aren't cryin', are you, kid?"

"I never cry," I said and, lifting my glasses, wiped the back of my hand against my eyes.

"Sung at Crumbly Hall yet?"

"It's *Carnegie* Hall," I snapped. I now knew that Carnegie Hall was in New York and that my idol, Judy Garland, had performed there. Had practically split the rafters with her belting out. "And, no, I'm not booked there, but keep checking with Ticketmaster."

I was also annoyed at Ardle for having startled poor old Mrs. Chewbley. Pantelli and I were very fond of her. Pantelli's regular piano teacher, Mrs. Grimsbottom, was a holy terror. As in, screeched at him for not practicing enough. Then, a few weeks ago, Mrs. Grimsbottom got sick, and Pantelli's mom found Mrs. Chewbley.

Mrs. Chewbley had turned out to be so very nice that Mother and Mr. Wellman, my agent, finally convinced me to start taking lessons. Mr. Wellman said, "You never know, Dinah. It might help you when you're older to be able to accompany yourself while you sing. Like Diana Krall."

Up to now, the only Krall I'd experienced was on my skin, at the thought of taking piano lessons with the dreaded Edna May Oliver exercise books and practices.

Pantelli liked Mrs. Chewbley even more than I did. *She actually puts up with my ranting about trees, Dinah. Can you believe it? Okay, so she lets out the occasional snore, but still...*

Anyhow, back to Ardle's sudden arrival. Mother rushed in, wrapped in a bathrobe and with a towel round her hair. "Mrs. Chewbley, what's with these repeated screams? I–"

She caught sight of Ardle.

"–AAAGGGHHH!"

There's nothing like the sight of other people getting upset to calm oneself down. I gulped down the last of the lump in my throat and announced, "Mother, this is Ardle McBean, an unsavory friend of Dad's."

Ardle laugh-coughed and winked at me. Jamming his cigarette in his mouth, he shoved the nicotine-yellow fingers of his right hand over the sill. "Sorry 'bout the abrupt arrival." Ardle grinned, displaying fewer teeth than I remembered. They were long and skinny, like him. "I saw the black-haired kid present himself at this window, and I thought maybe that's how they do things chizz Galloway."

"I think you mean the French word *chez*," Mrs. Chewbley

corrected rather crossly. She was pushing bobby pins back into place to re-secure her bird's nest bun, which had come undone with all her screaming.

"No, I mean 'chizz,'" said Ardle, and he laugh-coughed. I had to chomp my lower lip not to laugh with him. This was the kind of humor my friends and I found extremely witty.

Flushing, Mrs. Chewbley started gathering strawberry truffles from the floor and placing them atop the piano. Even slightly crushed, they looked good. But I had to restrain myself. Mother had this irritating rule about eating things off the floor.

Ardle winked at me. He knew exactly what I was thinking, I was sure of it. I had a feeling Ardle had never bothered much about irritating rules.

Mother ignored Ardle's outstretched hand. "You couldn't have been that good a friend of my husband's," she said coldly. "He never told me about you."

"I reckon I'm not the type he'd want to show off to his family," Ardle said agreeably.

With a sudden, lithe movement he hoisted himself on the sill. He used his still-outstretched hand to take three of the strawberry truffles Mrs. Chewbley had rescued. He piled them into his mouth all at once and winked at me again.

Ardle said, with his mouth full—another no-no for yours truly—"I just got outta the slammer, and I'm here to collect something Mike owed me."

Mother was edging toward the phone. I didn't have to be a psychic to know that the number in her mind was 9-1-1. "And what might that something be?" she asked.

Ardle displayed chocolate-covered teeth. "Eighty thousand dollars."

Eighty thousand dollars—Mike Galloway? *Our* Mike Galloway? Mother and I were statue-stiff with shock. Everyone knew that Dad never had any money at all. If he earned some, he spent it instantly on extravagant gifts for us or else booze.

"That's impossible," Mother finally blurted into the stunned silence.

"Nope." Ardle removed a much-creased piece of paper from his tattered denim jacket. "Got the IOU right here."

He unfolded it, and we saw, in Dad's untidy scrawl, *I'm keeping $80,000 for Ardle McBean—Michael Galloway,* with a seven-year-old date underneath.

Chapter Three

How a Prank Capped Dinah's Day

To my disappointment, Mother went ahead and punched in 9-1-1. Oh, I know that was the prudent thing to do, what with Ardle being an ex-con, but to me it was anti-climactic. Ardle scuttled away, though not before grabbing some more strawberry truffles. A fast exit, but a sweet one.

Two police officers showed up, took lots of notes and were very reassuring to Mother. If Ardle hassled us again, they'd charge him with extortion—a long word referring to his demand for the eighty thousand dollars.

"So, back to the Big House for him?" I said chattily to the nearest police officer, as one sleuth to another. Talbot, Pantelli and I had learned the term *big house* from all the old prison movies we enjoyed watching on Turner Classic Movies.

"Huh?" the officer said, puzzled—and Mother reminded me it was time for softball practice.

Whipping the bat round, I smashed the ball. Straight into the ground. Dirt flew.

Talbot St. John, who was helping teach girls' softball at our neighborhood park, stepped toward me from the pitcher's mound. "Interesting technique, Dinah," he observed. "Though awfully close to home plate, that would qualify as a live ball—and you might make it to first on the shock factor alone. The other team would be numb with amazement at a hitter who aimed for China."

"I have power," I defended myself. "The actual *range* will come later, I'm sure."

Talbot looked at me, his dark eyes skeptical. He made some notes on the chart attached to his clipboard. Talbot took his job as assistant instructor very seriously. As a matter of fact, Talbot took *life* very seriously—but I was working on that. There was hope for him yet.

On a rare athletic impulse, I'd got Mother to sign me up for these summer softball lessons, organized through our community center. Talbot had suggested it. He said he'd noticed that when he, Pantelli and I tossed a ball around, I had "potential."

Talbot pitched some more balls. More dirt flew. "You're making good progress, Dinah," Talbot said quietly, amid the guffaws from the girls on the bench.

Next up was Liesl Dubuque, the neighbors' niece.

Liesl, with raven hair and a pale pretty face that finished in a sharp chin, was staying next door for a year while her parents traveled.

Liesl and I did not like each other. Almost from the time she arrived on Wisteria Drive, she'd taunted me for being loud—which at first puzzled and then annoyed me because I'd always prided myself on my VOLUME. My voice was my heart, so in putting my voice down, she was putting down the essence of Dinah Mary Galloway.

Unfortunately, I was forbidden to insult Liesl or show her any sort of unpleasantness. The reason: A couple of months ago, in an e-mail prank, I'd tricked Liesl into chopping off that pitch-black hair she was so anxious to grow.

Hee hee.

Except that she who snickers last snickers best. Now Liesl could insult me all she wanted, while I had to maintain a saintly silence at all times. Or else, as Mother warned me, I'd be grounded for a year.

I took my place on the bench. Liesl was beckoning Talbot over from the pitcher's mound for a "personal consultation," as she called it. I weighed the immediate bliss of an insult or, even better, a running tackle against a year's worth of being grounded. If only Mother hadn't laid that on me. Why couldn't she be one of those irresponsible parents?

Talbot and Liesl consulted at the plate. This consisted of Liesl giggling shrilly and waving her hands a lot. After a while, Talbot returned to the pitcher's mound and tossed some balls at her. She hit them all smartly into the outfield. Liesl was one of the best athletes in school.

I applauded dutifully with the other girls. You had to appreciate someone's talent at something, even if they were otherwise thoroughly weasely.

At the opposite side of the park, under some maple trees, I glimpsed a patch of scarlet. It was a woman in a red dress, with a little boy clinging to her hand.

Normally I wouldn't have thought anything of this. The far end of the park was crammed with jungle gyms, swing sets and slides; moms and tots came here all the time. In our own kidlet days, Pantelli and I practically lived here. Pantelli, a tree fanatic from day one, used to sit in the sandbox, suck his knuckles and stare longingly at the maples.

But the woman in red was talking to—Ardle McBean! Talking intently too. The maple branches picked up a gust of breeze and waved in front of the woman, the boy and Ardle. I craned this way and that to focus on them.

The woman's free hand rose to her face. She was wiping tears away...

"You'll get a stiff neck with all that craning, Dinah," Talbot called.

"Now, Talbie, you're supposed to be paying attention to me," Liesl cooed, with just a bit of an edge to her voice.

She, too, spotted the flash of scarlet. "There's Mrs. Zanatta," Liesl tossed back at her buddies on the bench. "With that weird kid of hers who doesn't speak." They all laughed.

Poor little guy, I thought. Why doesn't he speak? I wished Liesl had that problem.

Madge showed up with a picnic basket crammed with brownies and lemonade. Liesl put on her good manners. She was impressed by Madge's cool glamor and was always asking her about makeup and fashions.

While everyone snacked, Talbot gave us pointers on smashing balls. "*Far away*," he added, with a look at me from under the dark forelock that Liesl had spent most of spring term drooling over.

Everyone laughed except me. "What's the matter?" Madge whispered to me. "Liesl Dubuque would kill to be the target of Talbot's teasing."

I stared at Madge. She laughed and gave me one of those annoying, older-sisterly knowing looks. "Dinah, you're clever, but you're not always smart."

"Here's your cap, Dinah," one of Liesl's friends giggled. She passed the cap, with its red-lettered *GARDEN PARK SOFTBALL ACES* on gray, along to me.

Liesl's pointy face thinned into an exclamation mark of panic. "Not now, Bertha," she snapped, glancing uneasily at Madge.

But I was already reaching for it. "I was wondering where this was," I said.

"This isn't the time," Liesl protested.

What was with her?

I jammed the cap on my head. And right away felt

something cold and gooey trickling into my scalp and down my face and ears.

Eggs.

"Apples."

I said the word somewhat indistinctly, as the shampoo Madge was working into my scalp was foaming around me and I didn't want to swallow any of it by mistake. My verbal analysis of the shampoo's scent glug-glugged down the sink along with the foam. I did like the apple smell, even if I was indignant about Liesl's prank.

And about Madge scrubbing my hair at the sink. I'd jumped in and out of the shower, but my sister took one look at my barely damp hair and said stronger measures were called for.

"I have to retaliate against Liesl," I'd objected.

"If you do, you'll be grounded for a year."

"That's so un—"

Before I could get the "fair" part out, my head was shoved in the sink. "Raw eggs are the toughest thing to remove," Madge said now, sounding suspiciously satisfied as she wrenched my hair about. "Somebody smeared raw eggs on Jack's windshield while he was holding a SOAC rally." SOAC stood for Spotted Owl Advocacy Committee, the student wildlife conservation group Jack was running this summer. "Jack had to take soap, water and a scrub brush to the glass before he could even think about driving."

"Please don't use the word 'SOAC' in these particular circumstances," I begged—and instantly had to cough out a gallon of apple shampoo foam. "And by the way, I don't think my *skull* needs cleaning."

"An appropriate choice of revenge," Madge mused, scrubbing cruelly on as if I hadn't spoken. "You trick Liesl into cutting her hair—and she tricks you into getting egg all over yours. Our Liesl isn't lacking in humor, even if it's a mean kind."

And Madge paused in wrench-washing my hair to toss back her own shiny, burnished red mane. Not that I could see this, but I knew my sister. She was very proud of her appearance. Who wouldn't be? Madge was slim, with vivid blue eyes and porcelain skin.

She was also decidedly *not* the type to get into feuds, even with weasels. Madge was very tidy with her life.

Then we heard a laugh-cough outside the kitchen window, and we knew a very untidy part of Dad's life was back again.

I sat on the living room sofa, toweling my hair. "If Mother sees you, she'll call the police," I warned Ardle, who was leaning in the window.

"No police, if ya don't mind. I already got somebody else after me." Ardle drew deeply, greedily on his cigarette, the way I knock back a bottle of water after a particularly grueling gym class. His addiction was gross but fascinating. Perhaps remembering what Dad had told him about secondhand smoke, Ardle exhaled sideways into the garden.

Madge had stomped away, refusing to have anything to do with Ardle. First, though, she'd icily informed Ardle that her fiancé was due any minute and would "deal with" him.

"Never say that to a card player," Ardle had joked, earning an angry sniff from my sister.

I, however, was curious about Ardle and kind of liked him. "Who's after you?"

"Who *isn't?*" Ardle rolled his eyes, and then he winced with pain. "Man, in my shape I shouldn't be exercising. Anyhow, Miss Carnegie Hall, I sure need to get my envelope back. It's gotta be in your dad's effects somewhere."

Effects was the word the police had used when they gave Mother what Dad had on him when he died. I still remembered the plastic bag they'd handed over: clothes, shoes, wallet, keys...A pretty meager summing up of a life.

"Dad didn't have eighty thousand dollars," I told Ardle. I'd heard Mother and Madge talking about it last night. They were totally bewildered by Ardle's claim.

"There's different ways of carryin' eighty grand," Ardle said cryptically.

Something came back to me, delivered up from my five-year-old self like the grubby dandelions I used to proudly present to Mother. "What you're looking for, is it something about a king?"

Ardle looked startled and then laugh-coughed. "Yer a sharp one. No wonder Mike was so proud of ya!"

"King of *what*, though?"

Ardle squinted at me through his billows of smoke. "Better for you I don't say, Miss Carnegie Hall. It's a dangerous secret to have. Some mighty ruthless folks would kill to find it out. That's why, fer seven long years, I've been silent," Ardle placed a yellow forefinger to his lips and dropped his voice, "as a fumigated cockroach."

From behind me, Madge said angrily, "You can share your revolting similes with the police, Mr. McBean. I'm calling nine-one-one."

A tediously predictable habit among the older Galloway women these days, in my view. "But Ardle was just..." I turned to indicate Dad's friend, but now only smoke hung over the windowsill. "Ardle?"

Beyond the smoke, a coughed reply. "I kin see I'm not welcome, Miss Carnegie Hall. Don't sweat it. Just check yer dad's effects, if you don't mind."

I ran out to the porch. By then Ardle was hotfooting it down the hill with the funny bouncing walk he had. A gray haze accompanied him, like the cloud of dust around Pigpen in *Peanuts*.

When he was halfway down the hill, a figure detached itself from behind our huge horse chestnut tree. A medium-height, stocky, brown-haired man in a black T-shirt and jeans. The brown hair, perfectly straight, flapped down the sides of his head in a bowl cut.

The man started down the Wisteria Drive sidewalk about twenty paces behind Ardle.

At one point Ardle paused, turned sideways and flung a cigarette butt into somebody's birdbath. The man dodged behind a Japanese cherry tree. When Ardle resumed walking, the man popped out again.

He was *following* Ardle.

Was he one of the "mighty ruthless folks" Ardle had referred to?

Declaring the smoke-infested living room a health risk, Mother and Madge sprayed it down with Lysol and shut the door. We received our next visitor, Jack's sister from down the alley, on our back porch.

Accepting a cup of tea from Mother, Geneva Rinaldi handed round the platter of butter tarts she'd brought over. Pretending I didn't notice Mother's and Madge's frowns, I helped myself to about six.

"...and our cousins from St. John, New Brunswick, of course," Mrs. Rinaldi prattled, scribbling in a large, coiled exercise book with the words *Wedding Planner* in silver on the cover. "Let's see now—they're allergic to chocolate, so I'm afraid no chocolate at your wedding, Madge." She chewed on her pencil. "Maybe sweetened tofu squares, instead?" She scribbled that down too.

"Um," said Madge.

However, the two women had both launched into an endless list of aunts, uncles and grandparents who ought to be invited. Madge, shut out of the discussion, gave me a helpless glance.

She and Jack had originally hoped for a small wedding, after which they'd settle into their studies—Madge at the Emily Carr Institute of Art and Design, Jack at the University of British Columbia, where he planned to study history and politics and eventually become a teacher.

"Mfglmtch," I said, my mouth full of tarts, by which I meant, *You'd think it was Mother and Mrs. Rinaldi's wedding from the way the two of them are carrying on.*

Normally each woman was quite sensible: Mother, shy and dreamy; Mrs. Rinaldi, good-humored and practical, like Jack.

In one of those weird, sisterly psychic moments, Madge thought of Jack at the same time. She whispered, "Jack can't make it here after all. He was just leaving, but somebody called 'LaFlamme' showed up at his office and insisted on seeing him. What kind of name is 'LaFlamme'?" Madge added crossly.

Mrs. Rinaldi peered distractedly up at Madge from the detailed notes she'd started making on pew flowers. "What's this about flames?" she demanded. Then Mrs. Rinaldi relaxed and chuckled. "Oh, you mean Jack's *on fire*, as it were. All men are like that before the marriage, m'dear. It soon changes! Why, my Luigi barely *looks* at me anymore."

Madge's eyes widened. She gaped at her future sister-in-law. Then she burst into tears and ran from the room.

"Oh, dear," Mother exclaimed, with a flash of her normal worried motherliness. "Perhaps I should go to her..."

Mrs. Rinaldi patted Mother's hand. "Typical bride behavior, Suzanne. Nerves of gossamer! If you want my opinion," and Jack's sister leaned forward confidently, "we'll get a lot more wedding work done on our own."

The two women were so busy I polished off most of the tarts on my own. Then, feeling a tad stuffed, I waddled round the room for exercise. "I'll tell you something *interesting*," I interrupted Mother and Mrs. Rinaldi, feeling that this planning nonsense had dragged on long enough. "Today, Liesl Dubuque emptied raw eggs on my head."

Mother and Mrs. Rinaldi stared. "Poor girl!" Mrs. Rinaldi exclaimed.

"Yes," I agreed, basking in this sympathy-for-the-victim attention, a rare experience for yours truly. "It took ages to wash—"

"Poor, poor Liesl," Mrs. Rinaldi continued, and Mother nodded along with her. "Dumped by her dad while he goes traipsing around the world with his new wife. And you know, Suzanne, wife number two isn't *quite* as young as he thinks..." The two women raised their eyebrows significantly at each other.

"The Dubuques can't be at all easy to live with," Mother said. "Not used to having children around, for one thing. That Mr. Dubuque, always shouting about the proper care of his tomato plants! Meanwhile, here's Liesl, trying desperately to fit in..."

I would have made retching noises, but at that moment

Pantelli's head popped into view over the windowsill. He was carefully removing leaves from a lilac bush for his leaf specimen collection. At the sight of Mrs. Rinaldi's butter tarts, he pointed to his mouth. Subtle, Pantelli was not.

Mother and Mrs. Rinaldi were engrossed in a debate about orange blossoms versus calla lilies. I raised a tart. Pantelli opened his mouth wide. I threw.

There are reasons besides lack of height that I don't make the basketball team. As with everything about me, it seems, my throw just had too much energy. The tart sailed right over Pantelli—

"AAAGGGHHH!"

Mother and Mrs. Rinaldi jumped up, clattering their teacups. "Nice one, Di," Pantelli commented.

On the sidewalk, massaging her eyelid, was the woman in red, Ardle's friend, Mrs. Zanatta.

Her little boy, like her, big eyed and chestnut haired, picked up the now-mashed tart and examined it—without saying anything. I remembered what Liesl, pardon me, *poor* Liesl, had said about him. *That weird kid of hers who doesn't speak.*

"Uh," I called to his mother, "this is a bit awkward. Sorry. I mis-aimed and—"

"Dinah, you will go upstairs this instant," Mother ordered.

Out of the side of his mouth, Pantelli stage-whispered to me, "That Zanatta dame has been gaping at your house for about ten minutes, Di. Think she's casing it for a break-in?"

Mother advanced to the window. Pantelli fled.

Chapter Four

Chestnuts and Cobwebs

Spotting me at the Trout Lake Farmers' Market, which we Galloways trooped down to every Saturday, the regular guitarist immediately strummed and sang:

Dinah, is there anyone finer,
In the state of Carolina...

It's the song I was named after. Dad used to sing it to Mother in the days when they held hands in cafés along Commercial Drive, put their quarters together to split a cappuccino and dreamed of all kinds of wonderful possibilities.

Well, possibilities didn't always work out, but music kept on. I sang along with the guitarist, and quite a few people tossed coins in his open guitar case.

The gleaming white market stalls were filled with cheeses, fresh produce, pottery, jewelry, pickles, seafood and baked nummies.

Madge, Jack, Mother and I drifted from vendor to vendor, buying from almost everyone and filling up our backpacks. Beyond the market hubbub, dogs chased each other around sparkling Trout Lake. The perfect day.

"You sure you want to go to Toronto?" Jack teased Madge. His gray eyes studied her wistfully. "Three whole days away from you! I don't know if I can stand it."

"But a train trip," said Mother dreamily. "Trains, such marvelous settings for Alfred Hitchcock films...One thinks of *The Lady Vanishes*..."

"And then one switches one's mind away from it," I said firmly. I wrenched a huge radish off one of the bunches she'd bought and bit into it for maximum *kee-rrrunch* effect.

Mother was the bookish type, always lapsing into literary references. Since she'd started going out with Jon Horowitz, a play director, she'd added film references to her literary ones. Jon was mad for old movies. He and Mother went to repertory theaters to see old movies at least once a week.

"Or of course *Strangers on a Train*," Mother added.

"*Mother*," Madge and I said crossly.

She laughed. "I'm sure the train trip will be soothing and serene, not Hitchcockian at all."

"Er—yes." Over by the vendor selling ostrich meat, as well as fluffy ostrich-feathered pens and key chains, I saw Talbot and his mom. Liesl Dubuque had just wriggled up to chat with him. How *could* he be so friendly with her, after the egg incident?

With determination, I made myself look away. "So tell me," I said to Mother, "do you find Mrs. Zanatta unsavory in any way?"

"Certainly not," Mother replied, astonished. "I've met her in the park a few times, and she seems very nice and quiet. Her little boy is very shy. A kindergartener, I believe. I wonder..."

I cut Mother off before she could utter something do-goodish, like suggesting we invite the Zanattas over for tea. "But what do you actually *know* about this woman?"

"Well...they haven't lived here long." Mother's forehead crinkled into a suspicious frown. "You're not involved in another mystery, are you, Dinah? Because you're really too busy to be—"

"Great, cake!" I exclaimed hastily. Jack had just handed us pieces of sweet, sticky, matrimonial squares, a specialty at the Small Pleasures baking stall. I crammed in the crumbly, buttery, dates-and-golden-syrup-filled square all at once so I wouldn't have to answer Mother.

Jack and Madge, meanwhile, were—get this—feeding pieces of their cake *to each other*. Yech.

"Dinah, we leave in two days," Talbot said. "I'm not sure this is the best time to be taking a jaunt down memory lane."

He, Pantelli and I were crouching in the low doorway to the Galloway attic. I put up a hand and nudged aside a wheel-sized cobweb. "Mother and Madge are out. This is our one chance to look in Dad's effects for something worth eighty thousand smackeroos."

I let the cobweb fall on Talbot's face. "Of course, if you have someone you'd *rather* be spending time with…"

He shoved the cobweb aside and we glared at each other.

Pantelli was gazing out the window at the top branches of our horse chestnut tree. "A rare, satisfying, top-down perspective of *Aesculus hippocastanum*," he observed and made his way to the window through an obstacle course of trunks and boxes.

Talbot informed me coldly, "I'd like to have a rare, satisfying perspective of *fairness* from you, Dinah Galloway. The reason I was talking to Liesl at the market was to warn her. I said any more pranks—eggs-asperating or other—and she'd be booted off the Garden Park Softball Aces."

"Oh," I said. "Well, I may have been a *bit* hasty."

We grinned at each other and everything was all right again.

Struggling with the window latch, Pantelli called back, "As *aesculus* comes from *esca*, or 'food,' there's some thought that the name was given as a joke. Horse chestnuts are way too bitter to eat, unlike sweet chestnuts." *Cr-r-r-eak*! Pantelli flung the window open.

"Toxic and poisonous," Pantelli said with satisfaction. "They contain aesculin, a bitter compound that breaks down blood proteins. As in, poisons you. Not fatally, but you'd be so sick you'd *wish* you were dead."

He leaned over the windowsill. Magnifying glass in hand, he was inspecting one of the chestnut gourds that gleamed like green lamps all over the tree. In another month they'd start falling to the ground and splitting. We'd scoop out the smooth, mahogany-colored chestnuts and roll them around in our hands like dice, enjoying their smooth coolness.

"Poisonous if you eat a lot of leaves, that is," Pantelli explained, pulling a branch toward him. "The effect all depends on the dose. Ironically, in small doses, and mixed with other ingredients, the plant is useful in the treatment of stuff like hardened arteries, leg ulcers and frostbite."

The top half of Pantelli was over the sill by now. Talbot and I traded uneasy glances. "How about for the treatment of people who fall out of windows?" Talbot called.

"I'm *fine*. You guys don't understand what it is to be a dendrologist."

"Dendrologist?" I repeated. "Is that someone who makes dentures?"

"Of course not." Pantelli's voice floated back to us, insulted. "It's someone who studies trees."

Exchanging shrugs, Talbot and I began examining the labels Mother had Magic-Markered on boxes.

Most of the boxes contained either photos or Madge's and my schoolwork and report cards. The boxes were jammed between broken lamps and chairs that we couldn't bring ourselves to throw out, and relatives' presents none of us wanted, like the smiling brass woman whose ten hands each balanced a candleholder.

"How do we know which box has your dad's effects?" asked Talbot. He examined a grim portrait of a Galloway great-uncle. "Hey, this old guy scowls just like you do, Dinah."

"Very funny." I eased between stacks of boxes. The problem was I had no idea where Mother had stashed Dad's effects. I knew, from something Madge had once said, that Mother had put them away as quickly as possible because they were too painful to look at.

Pantelli had pulled a leaf off the nearest branch and was poring over it. "Reasonably healthy," he pronounced. And then he mused, "The real puzzler is why the 'horse' in 'horse chestnut.' Possibly 'cause the plant has been used in mixtures for curing horses and cattle of coughs."

Talbot and I were busy shifting boxes back, forth and sideways. "I dunno if this is getting us anywhere," said Talbot. "I feel like we're playing Tetris." His dark eyes narrowed at me in sudden suspicion. "Are you sure your mom said it was okay to do this?"

"Er..." This was a sticky point. The way I'd explained it to Talbot, Mother hadn't refused to let us look. Which she hadn't, since I'd never asked her.

Pantelli continued, "Some researchers think the 'horse' part is from the Welsh word *gwres*, meaning hot and fierce-tasting. That is, a flavor sensation you'd want to avoid."

I snapped my by-now extremely dusty fingers. "'Avoid'! That's it! Mother wanted to avoid seeing Dad's effects. So she would've put them somewhere *out of the way*."

Talbot and I stopped moving the boxes on the floor around. "Out of the way" in this attic could only mean the high shelf that ran around the room.

We squinted past the cobwebs that were strung from section to section of the shelf like telephone wires. "*DINAH'S VALIBLE COMIX*," Talbot read aloud from the side of one small box. "*IF U THROW AWAY, PRIPAR TO DIE.*"

"Never mind those," I said. Being height-challenged, I scrambled up on one of the floor boxes for a better look.

At the window, Pantelli called, "Hi, Mrs. Chewbley! Whatcha doin'?"

Mrs. Chewbley's rueful laugh echoed up to us. "I'm looking for my glasses. I dropped them somewhere when I finished Dinah's piano lesson earlier today."

I spotted a sealed plastic bag. Even through the cobwebs I could read the typewritten label. *Michael Galloway: Effects.*

I reached, and then I hesitated.

"You sure you want to see them, Dinah?" Talbot asked quietly.

I heaved a big breath. "Yeah. Yeah, we have to."

But once Talbot placed the bag in my hands, I hesitated again. I wasn't at all sure I wouldn't break into a blubberfest on opening the bag. So, putting off the moment, I strolled to the window to shout my own hello down to Mrs. Chewbley.

"I've been practicing a lot," I assured her.

"Um...great," she said, hunched over our lawn. "Is your mother home, Dinah?"

"No, she's working," I replied.

"Oh, right. I forgot." Mrs. Chewbley laughed. She began prattling about her forgetfulness.

Life being short, I was about to smile politely and withdraw from the window. Then, to Mrs. Chewbley's left, two of the cedar trees bunched at the side of our garden wriggled. Amid their branches, a face appeared.

A man's face, staring coldly, speculatively, at our house.

I recognized his bowl haircut. The man who'd been following Ardle!

Chapter Five

Bowl Cut's Hair-Raising Entrance

"Hey you!" I yelled indignantly. "Whaddya want?"

Talbot gave me a nudge. "That's not the nicest way to talk to Mrs. Chewbley."

"*No*, him!" I pointed at the bowl-cut man.

Two things happened simultaneously. Bowl Cut's face, round and white like a dinner plate, withdrew into the branches. And I jarred Pantelli's outstretched hand so that he dropped his magnifying glass. Down, down it toppled to *boink!* Mrs. Chewbley on the head. She collapsed on some fallen horse chestnut leaves.

We all raced downstairs, me clutching Dad's effects, and Pantelli moaning about how his expensive magnifying glasses kept getting broken around me. (His last magnifying glass had cracked when we were sleuthing the month before, in North Vancouver.)

This one, however, was crack-free. Disentangling it from her bird's nest bun, Mrs. Chewbley chuckled weakly. "Lucky I have so much thick, unkempt hair. It acts as padding."

We helped her to her feet and into the Galloway living room. "I'll make you some tea," I offered. Tea was the Galloway cure for everything.

Talbot then charged back out to investigate whether Bowl Cut really was an intruder or just a Dubuque friend or relative with a strange fondness for cedar trees.

I left Pantelli inspecting Mrs. Chewbley's scalp through his magnifying glass. "No injury," he reported, "but have you considered using Head and Shoulders?"

I put the kettle on with tons of water because I wanted time to go through the plastic bag. With hands that shook only slightly, I removed Dad's folded clothes, including the red and black flannel shirt I used to love rubbing my cheek against. I stroked the shirt for a moment, and then I laid all his clothes and his shoes on the kitchen counter.

The kitchen was very quiet. Through the open window, on a hint of a breeze, the leaves of the Japanese cherry out back fluttered and whispered.

Dad, I thought. And for an instant I could see him: warm grin, black eyes sparkling with enthusiasm.

The leaves stopped fluttering, and Dad faded. It was hot and still again.

I made myself think practically. Ardle, and whoever was after him, weren't interested in Dad's clothes. The eighty

grand, in whatever form, had to be among the other things
in the bag.

I found a black leather wallet with some bills, coins
and credit cards inside. Gleaming through a plastic casing
was a photo of our family in front of the Pacific National
Exhibition's wooden roller coaster. The one Dad and I had
gone on again and again, but Mother and Madge had been
scared of. A passerby had snapped us.

And inside the money pocket—an unsealed stamped
envelope.

Was this the envelope Ardle had meant? It had nothing
inside. There wasn't even an address, though Dad had
scrawled our return one on the back flap.

I held up the envelope.

"Hey, cool stamp!" Pantelli marched in with his magnifying glass. One day Talbot and I were going to have to
unweld it from his hand.

Pantelli pored over the envelope, admiring the stamp—a
huge gold-bordered one, featuring an elk in a meadow and
the words *Celebrating Canada's wildlife* in gold lettering
below. "And not franked, either. Betcha this is worth
something."

"Eighty thousand dollars?" I said doubtfully. "It's only
seven years old."

Mrs. Chewbley ambled in, vainly trying to push all her
loose strands of hair into place. So much for my idea of
some quality time alone.

"An eighty-thousand-dollar stamp?" She peered through

the magnifying glass and laughed. "It's a nice one, but I doubt you'd get even eighty *cents* for it at a philatelist's. A stamp collector's," she clarified, in response to Pantelli's and my vocabulary-challenged expressions. "As you say, Dinah, it's too recent."

Mrs. Chewbley noticed my crestfallen expression. She smiled kindly. "You could ask about it, though. After all, what do I know? I'm just a dithery old piano teacher."

The kettle gave a shrill whistle. I set four mugs out beside the wallet, envelope and keys. Then I rummaged for Mother's loose-leaf Darjeeling tea. I couldn't see the tea strainer anywhere, so I grabbed the colander and began dumping spoonfuls of tea leaves into it. Pouring boiling water over them, I passed the colander back and forth over mugs. Lots of water splashed on the counter, but hey. We creative types are into improvising.

I was glad Mother and Madge weren't there. They always acted so...uneasy when I did things in the kitchen.

Oh, I know, I know. Technically the colander should have been washed. I'd plucked it from the sink, where bits of cooked pasta were clinging to it. Still, I didn't think Mrs. Chewbley had to look so dismayed. She had to be used to me and my little ways by now.

"It's *reasonably* clean," I defended myself.

The piano teacher let out a piercing scream.

"Look, Mrs. Chewbley, I think one can carry this hygiene thing a bit—"

Pantelli elbowed me. I turned.

Bowl Cut loomed grimly through the open window. He stretched over the counter, reaching for the envelope...

Pantelli and I each grabbed a side of the window and shoved down hard.

Bowl Cut withdrew his hand, but not fast enough. The window landed on his thumb. "YEOWWW!"

"I know that man," Mrs. Chewbley exclaimed. She was so excited that her hair was popping out of its pins again. "I've seen him skulking behind bushes and trees, up and down Wisteria Drive. A prowler! We must call the police immediately." She grabbed the nearest phone, which happened to be Madge's neon red and yellow cell—my sister was more into the fashion of communications than the actual function—and began jabbing at buttons. "Oh dear, I never could get the hang of these newfangled contraptions..."

I grabbed the phone from her. There was no time to waste, because Bowl Cut was slowly wrenching his thumb back out from under the window.

Then Talbot appeared outside.

"EEEE-YAWWW!" He hurled himself shoulder-first into Bowl Cut. Both Talbot and Pantelli were huge Jackie Chan fans.

Lurching, Bowl Cut smashed against the side of our house. His trapped thumb was yanked free from between the window and sill, rattling the pane so hard it cracked.

Cradling his bloodied thumb, Bowl Cut staggered away.

Chapter Six

Laughs, Coughs and a Screech of Brakes

"Talbot?!" Mother said disbelievingly. She gaped at the broken windowpane. "*Talbot* did this? Talbot the good?"

"Talbot the good?" I repeated. Mother was making my dark-eyed, and at this moment very apologetic, buddy sound like some ancient Saxon king.

"Yeah," Pantelli said gleefully. "A first! Who woulda thought? And, man, that is some pane crack." He leaned over to examine it with his magnifying glass. "Not unlike the shape of the St. Lawrence River. Hey!" He pointed to an oblong space where a chunk of glass had fallen out. "That could be Lake Ontario."

"I'm really sorry, Mrs. Galloway," Talbot said, unhappy under his dark forelock, which, in the circumstances, appeared even more soulful than usual. "I'll pay for it myself. I'll go home right now, get my bank card and bike to the bank."

"There was *an intruder*," I interrupted. "It's not your fault, Talbot. If it's anyone's, it's mine."

Mother let out a huge sigh that ruffled the beet leaves sticking out of the grocery bag she'd just brought home. "*Your* fault, Dinah? Now that's territory I'm more familiar with."

"There *was* an intruder," Mrs. Chewbley chimed in through a mouthful of cheese. Espying a package of old cheddar in the grocery bag, she'd removed it and sliced herself a large piece. And without asking! Mrs. Chewbley was definitely a woman after my own heart. Or stomach, anyhow.

"Most likely this man is casing houses for break-ins," the piano teacher continued. She wagged a fairly substantial cheese slice at us. "Best always to double-check that you've locked doors and windows." She polished off the cheese.

"*I* think," I began—and then I stopped. It might be better if Mother and Madge didn't know I'd rifled through Dad's effects.

I'd bundled Dad's clothes back to the attic before Mother and Madge returned. The envelope I'd stuffed in my duffel bag. I saw no alternative but to take it with me on the train and pore over it some more. Who knew, maybe Dad had written a message on it in invisible ink.

Madge, always more suspicious than Mother, regarded me through narrowed lupine-blue eyes. "You think what, Dinah?"

I flashed my best phony bared-teeth smile (patent pending) at her in return. "Probably we should call the police and give them a full description of this mysterious bowl-cut intruder."

"Good idea," Mother said, smiling at me. "I'm glad that for once you haven't decided to pursue this mystery yourself."

I stretched my insincere smile wider. As long as Mrs. Chewbley didn't mention that we'd been discussing elk stamps and philatelists...

But the piano teacher gave no sign of doing that. She plugged in the kettle for fresh tea and reached into the grocery bag for a packet of fudge Oreos. Her mind was on food. The best people's were, I decided and felt very fond of Mrs. Chewbley, even if she didn't appreciate my loud piano-playing.

Softball in the park again, the last practice before we boarded the train for Toronto. The other girls on the bench were all cooing about how exciting it was.

Except for Liesl. Though it was her turn to bat, she was slathering on bright red lip-gloss. "Just one more layer," she called to Talbot, who was shaking his head at her.

The funny thing was, much as I'd longed to appear

on *Tomorrow's Cool Talent*, I didn't want to go. Not till I'd found the eighty grand Ardle claimed we had. Not till Bowl Cut was caught.

The police had promised to look out for him. "Unless he visits the hairdresser any time soon, he should stand out like the sore thumb you gave him," Mother had assured me.

I twirled my cap on my forefinger. (Laundered, it was now egg-free.) If only I didn't have to leave Vancouver. Not yet. Not *yet*.

And "Black Socks," the song I'd been belting out when I was five and Ardle had knocked on the door, came back to me:

Someday I think I will wash them,
But something keeps telling me
Don't do it yet,
Not yet, not yet...

A cloud of smoke encircled me, followed by a laugh-cough.

"Ardle!" I exclaimed, jumping. "That's weird. I was just thinking about you."

Ardle grinned. His lips were pursed as if he were trying to hide his few lopsided teeth. "Checked out your house, but no one there. So I thought I'd stroll down to the park, catch some rays and wait fer a while. And here ya are...Whoa, that's a gigantic sore yer friend's got."

He peered over his cigarette and down the bench to Liesl, who'd finally finished layering on the lip-gloss. Her mouth was a round, red sheen, like the planet Mars.

"Liesl the Weasel's no friend of mine," I replied sourly. "You won't believe what she did to me the other day."

And I blabbed the whole incident to him. What can I say? Sometimes my lips have sneakers tied to them.

"I'll take care of this fer ya," Ardle promised, adding ominously, "Nobody behaves like that to a kid of Mike Galloway's." He marched, in his bobbing-up-and-down way, past the bench and alongside the baseball field.

"Um, wait," I began uneasily.

Talbot pitched. Liesl walloped the ball. Ardle leaped, smacked his knees and laugh-coughed hysterically.

Talbot and Liesl turned and stared.

"Ooo, sorry," Ardle apologized, wiping his eyes.

More pitches, more wallops, more leaps and laugh-coughs.

"Now *look*, buddy," said Talbot. He started toward Ardle.

Ardle held up his hands. "Sorry—it's a condition I have."

Talbot hesitated. On his sensitive features, doubt struggled with his natural good manners toward an adult. "Maybe you could laugh and cough somewhere else," he suggested.

"Sure, buddy! With McBean, you kin McCount on it."

Right. When Talbot made his next pitch, Ardle was still there. This time Liesl, her eyes panicky above her Mars-like mouth, freaked and missed completely.

If only—if *only*—Talbot hadn't glanced at me just then.

Though I was chomping down on the inside of one cheek to keep from laughing, I couldn't help letting a smile flit across my face...

Ardle cheered *my* hits, which was a bit of a stretch. He sure was loyal to the memory of my dad.

When I'd finished and was slinking away from Talbot's accusing this-guy's-a-*friend*-of-yours? expression, Ardle announced he had to go for fresh "smokes."

"How many packs a day do you go through?" I demanded disapprovingly.

"Measuring by tens or dozens?" He bobbed off, laugh-coughing, past the wading pool and surrounding hedge at the far corner of the park.

An ancient, dented gray Buick careened around the park, past the softball diamond, toward that far corner.

From behind the hedge, a figure sprang up. I couldn't see his dinner-plate face, but I didn't need to. I'd recognize that bowl cut anywhere.

Ardle started to cross the street.

The gray Buick screeched toward Ardle. Bowl Cut leaped and reached for Ardle.

"WATCH OUT!" I yelled, flailing my arms.

Too late. The Buick slammed into Ardle, sending him Frisbee-like through the air to smash on the sidewalk.

The Buick tore down the street. It swung left on busy Broadway. Amid the angry honkings of other motorists, it disappeared.

I was already running to Ardle. I could see Bowl Cut bending over Ardle's inert body, reaching inside his jacket pockets. Searching for the eighty-thousand-dollar king, I thought.

The singing exercises I had to do each week for my voice instructor paid off. Though out of breath, I was able to yell at Bowl Cut.

"AAAGGGHHH!"

Okay, not overly articulate, but Bowl Cut did whip round. "AAAGGGHHH!" I re-hollered. I splashed through the wading pool, causing waves that capsized a cute toddler's plastic ship. He burst into loud, uncute wails. His mom was on her cell, 9-1-1-ing it. "Terrible accident...Garden Park," she jabbered.

I sprinted the last few yards over to Ardle. He was sheet-pale. His breath came out in ragged gasps. Kneeling beside him, I grasped his nicotine-stained fingers. "Hold on for the ambulance," I begged. Had someone been there to tell Dad that after his car accident? My eyes swam with tears, which plopped onto my glasses' frames.

I glared blurrily at Bowl Cut. "You did this," I accused. "Is eighty grand that important? IS IT?"

Bowl Cut's round face soared up and out of sight like a wayward ping-pong ball. He ran up to Broadway.

An ambulance, a fire truck and two police cars screamed up to us in a splash of red lights.

"Hey, Di." Talbot knelt beside me and put his arm around my shoulders. "Hey," he said.

He held out a folded white handkerchief. I blew my nose into it with my usual deafening honks. I was suddenly glad for Talbot's well-brought-up conscientiousness, which included carrying clean hankies around and somehow not minding what a doofus I was.

Ardle, who hadn't been at all well brought up, winked at me weakly from the stretcher he was being shifted onto. I bet he had his good points too—more challenging to find, that's all. If I ever *had* the chance to find them now.

"I'll be okay," he croaked. "Yer a good kid. Mike Galloway's kid. Crumbly Hall, huh?" And then, incredibly, he managed a laugh-cough.

As the ambulance attendants hoisted him, Ardle's lean features stiffened. "Careful," he wheezed, clenching my hand. "Be careful of ..." And with his other hand he gestured in the direction Bowl Cut had fled. "Mighty dangerous."

He shut his eyes. The attendants lifted the stretcher.

"But who *is* Bowl Cut?" I demanded. In a minute Ardle would be in the ambulance. Already a policewoman's hands were on my shoulders, prying me away. "And who's this king?"

"A king, yeah. A king who lost his head," Ardle muttered on a cigarette-smoky breath.

"Huh?"

Ardle wagged his head feverishly. "Naw. Shouldn't have said that much to ya. Too dangerous..."

The attendants heaved Ardle away.

"Poor fellow," the policewoman tsked. "Imagine babbling out such nonsense! Dazed by the accident, I shouldn't wonder."

The doors closed behind Ardle, and the ambulance shrieked off.

Chapter Seven

A Peanut-Butter Voice Creates a Sticky Situation

I rang up Vancouver General Hospital with advice about Ardle. "Put him near an open window. He needs lots of fresh air. He's a smoker," I finished ominously.

"But I'm just the receptionist," the young man on the other end bleated.

"Fine. Put me through to surgery."

Mother grabbed the phone and hung it up. "Dinah, I promise you we'll check in a while. It's much too soon to—"

Brrring!

I lunged for the phone again. Mother, Madge and Jack, at the kitchen table knocking back cups of tea, exchanged despairing glances through the Earl Grey-scented steam. Or maybe it was Darjeeling or Ceylon steam. The three of them had become tea fanatics and grew quite tiresome with their discussions of hint of vanilla here, touch of red pepper there and so on.

"*Hello*!?" I shouted into the phone. It's good to take the upper hand immediately in calls, I find.

A feeble croak limped out of the receiver. "Please, Dinah. I'm already ill—no need to deafen me."

"Mr. Wellman!"

"I can't go to Toronto with you," my agent rasped back. "The way I feel, the only trip I'll be taking anytime soon is to the graveyard. Some fool showed up today wanting to be taken on as a client. Guess what the idiot's specialty was. *Whistling*. Like I could get bookings for a *whistler*."

"How about for *Whistler's Mother*?"

The rasp turned into a growl. "No jokes, Dinah Mary Galloway. This whistling idiot had the flu—and breathed all over my lunch as we chatted. I should sue, I tell ya. *Sue*."

Mother started up from the table. "Did I hear my name?"

I handed the phone to her. "Hi, Suzanne," I heard Mr. Wellman hoarsely bark. "You won't believe..."

I fled. Sorry as I felt for Mr. Wellman, I wanted to pore over Dad's envelope some more. Was there any clue to the eighty grand on it? And what had Ardle meant by *a king who lost his head*?

As I climbed the stairs, a plaintive cry from Madge echoed through the house: "What? I have to escort Dinah, Talbot and Pantelli to Toronto—*alone*?"

"It's not that bad," Jack told my sister as I sat on my suitcase to force it shut, and he fastened the latches. "I mean, Dinah, Talbot and Pantelli aren't animals."

Madge looked up from the very tidy, compartmentalized suitcase she was about to close with a slim hand. "Jack, their ages range from twelve to thirteen. You know very well that's the most gruesome possible stage in a human being's life. The age when kids go through," she shuddered, "transition issues. Emotional changes."

Then she noticed herself in the hall mirror: slim, porcelain-skinned, and impossibly, for that hot August day, cool and elegant in a sleeveless indigo top and matching Capri pants. She gave a satisfied smile. "I was a model twelve- and thirteen-year-old. Quiet, well-behaved, causing no trouble whatsoever. All the teachers commented on it."

Jack shot her a fond, exasperated glance. Then, hoisting my case, he frowned. "This feels suspiciously heavy, Dinah."

I shrugged. "One day they'll make lighter PlayStations, I'm sure."

"You packed a *Pl*–? Remove it pronto, young woman."

I frowned back at him. Like, c'mon. A PlayStation was a must-have accessory when traveling. "I'm being restrained," I defended myself. "I told Pantelli *he'd* have to bring the TV."

"Not after I phone Mrs. Audia, he won't," Jack said firmly.

Jack was getting awfully bossy, I reflected, and he wasn't even a member of the family yet. Not officially. In fact, I sometimes wondered how their wedding could ever occur, what with Mother and Mrs. Rinaldi complicating it more each day with their "plans."

Anyhow, Jack and Madge planned to live, if or when the wedding did happen, in our long-neglected basement. Madge had sketched designs, and she and Jack were renovating the basement bit by bit every day. Their downstairs suite was going to be pretty nice, with French doors opening out onto our lilac-fragrant, blackberry-wild garden. And I was delighted they wouldn't be moving away—yay!

Except at moments like now, when Jack was being unreasonable. "We're talking two PlayStation-less weeks," I muttered, dragging the machine out. Okay, so the case was now lighter, but no way I'd admit that. "I'll have withdrawal symptoms," I warned.

Nobody heard me. Jack and Madge, holding hands, had one of those sweetheart-only, glued gazes going that normal people find extremely annoying. Jack was saying, "I, by contrast, was not a model twelve- or thirteen-year-old. Adults despaired of me until a couple of teachers inspired me to think about what I could be, as opposed to what I was. Yup, I used to be pretty beastly, all right. Then look what happened: The beast ended up with the beauty."

Amazingly they were oblivious to my barfing noises. Hmm. I must be slipping.

They didn't hear, either, the rhythm-and-blues set that

was the sound of Jack's cell going off. Ever helpful, I grabbed it from the hall table.

"Psychiatric ward," I said into it.

"I beg your—is this Jack French's number?" inquired a female voice, smooth and gravelly at the same time, like creamy peanut butter with chunks.

In my opinion, the very-much-engaged Jack French should not be receiving calls from women with chunky peanut-butter voices. "Who are *you*?" I demanded.

"Is this—" The voice faltered. "This isn't Madge, is it? Er—oops, wrong number." Click!

My disapproval rating of Jack shot way up. I narrowed my eyes at him, not that he noticed. He was still in tender-gaze mode with Madge.

Whom all at once I felt very protective of. Jack was keeping Peanut-Butter Voice, whoever she was, a secret from Madge. Fine behavior for a fiancé. Poor Madge!

Chapter Eight
Jack and the Beanstalk

I did a mini tap dance on the white marble floor of Pacific Central Station. Above me the spindly hands of the brass and glass clock tucked themselves together over the six. Almost time to go! I pictured the vast spaces of Canada we'd be traveling through—dramatic Rockies, prairies with their endless skies—and picked up the pace of my tap dance.

Uh-oh. Mother, having tearfully hugged Madge good-bye for the ninetieth time, was turning amid sobs to me again. Enough was enough. I dodged behind the clock.

Passengers filed past, toward the departures sign and the platform beyond. Some of them hurried, brushing against me crossly for being in their way. The sleek, stainless steel Gold-and-Blue would be carrying three hundred passengers in all.

Including one rough one. My left arm was yanked

backward. "Ow," I protested and glared round, massaging my shoulder.

The colored rope of my knitted rainbow purse, made by Madge for me last Christmas, flopped to the ground. The purse itself was gone. Snatched!

"Pickpockets everywhere," sniffed a beanstalk-tall conductor, whom an indignant Jack more or less tackled about my missing purse. The conductor wrinkled his long nose and flapped his rubbery lips. "One has to be *careful*," he admonished, looking way down at me as if it were my fault.

"What did you have in the purse, Dinah?" questioned Madge, clutching her own tan bag covered with black C's—for Chanel, her favorite designer—closer to her.

"Travel essentials," I mourned. "A Deathstalkers comic. And the *Block Watch for Dummies* book I'm writing."

"I'll check the Lost and Found," Mother suggested.

"Once the thief realizes there's nothing valuable inside, he or she will toss the purse away," Madge said witheringly.

I almost retorted. But then, remembering Peanut-Butter Voice, I laid a soothing hand on her arm. "I'm sorry our departure has to be like this, so upsetting for everyone. I'm sure you'll find the trip itself relaxing."

Jack, busy berating the conductor, stopped to gape at me.

"It's—it's okay," Madge said weakly.

At the train, Beanstalk forbade Jack's accompanying us on board to say good-bye. "Rules," Beanstalk informed us haughtily.

"No!" Madge exclaimed in dismay. Deprived of a whole extra minute together, she and Jack clutched each other. Gad, you'd have thought they were parting for three decades, not *three days*.

Then, to my own dismay, they began smooching.

"Jack, how will I bear it—"

"Madge, I'll miss you madly—"

Thinking of Peanut-Butter Voice, I snorted.

Jack tore his gaze away from Madge and looked at me, puzzlement glinting in his gray eyes.

"Dinah!" Mother called loudly. I hate when she does that: everyone looks and realizes it's *my* maternal unit being so embarrassing. She panted up to us and thrust my now-strapless rainbow purse at me. "Found it on the floor!"

I checked inside. Nothing missing. Since I rarely carried a purse, I was in the habit of storing really valuable stuff, like money and my school cafeteria card, and now Dad's envelope, in pockets. I slipped my hand in a sweater pocket and clasped the envelope. Yup, still safely there. Whatever *was* there that a thief would want.

An enormous twittering arose ahead of us. "Dear me...gracious..."

Mrs. Chewbley, who'd agreed at the last moment to be our substitute chaperone, was wedged in a train door with Beanstalk. Her large, flowered-print bag was jammed between them.

"Madam, please!' Beanstalk snapped, trying to wiggle free.

Madge, trim and pretty in a navy jacket and skirt, massaged her forehead as if a headache were developing. "Of all the people to replace Mr. Wellman as my co-chaperone," she sighed. "A woman as disorganized as *that*." Madge waved her left hand at the piano teacher. She waved it for quite a while, earning odd looks from passersby—but I knew it was because she liked admiring the twinkles of her diamond engagement ring.

"Shhh, Madge," Mother admonished. "Edwina's doing us a favor. Besides, being able to use Mr. Wellman's ticket gives Edwina a chance to travel. I don't think she could afford this on her own."

Mrs. Chewbley was now chirping advice to Beanstalk on how best to unstick themselves. "It might be best if you relaxed, young man. So long as you remain tense, we're likely to stay stuck in this doorway for hours."

Pantelli and Talbot, who'd arrived just after us, staggered up. As well as their suitcases, they were weighted down with a Softie Toilet Paper carton (Pantelli) and a guitar case (Talbot). People paused during boarding to laugh loudly at the toilet paper carton. "I have *leaf samples* in here," Pantelli informed them coldly. "I'm a dendrologist."

"A denture-ologist? Excellent," exclaimed a plump, salt-and-pepper-haired, pink-cheeked woman fanning herself with a *Welcome to the Gold-and-Blue Train Company!* brochure. Drawing back her lips, she displayed askew upper dentures to Pantelli. "I could use your help with these, sonny. I made the mistake of knocking back a pound of saltwater taffy yesterday and warped 'em." With the tip of her tongue, she shoved the dentures more firmly into place—*click*!

Pantelli ignored her. "Try a crowbar," he suggested to Mrs. Chewbley and Beanstalk. Along with his interest in trees, Pantelli fancied himself a logical, problem-solving scientist. "What we need here is some leverage."

"What we need here is some dieting," complained Beanstalk, with an unkind glance at Mrs. Chewbley's stomach. He then glared angrily at Jack, who was shaking with laughter.

"I've worked out a plan," Talbot announced. Grasping the flowered-print bag's handle, he leaned back. "Heave!" he shouted and began to pull. "HEAVE!"

The flowered-print bag came away in his hands, the zipper breaking open to disgorge the contents, including a red flannel nightgown, at least a dozen romance novels with shapely fainting women on the covers, and boxes and boxes of chocolate creams.

Inside the train, Beanstalk got a proper look at Madge for the first time. His long face softened into a silly smirk. "Ooo, a young lass like you shouldn't have to carry heavy items," he cooed—and removed the small black and beige Chanel case from her hand.

Talbot and Pantelli, huffing and puffing with their suit-cases, glared at Beanstalk. "How about helping us young lads?" Talbot inquired.

The conductor curved his rubbery back forward and down until he was eyeball to eyeball with Talbot. "As assistant head conductor, I am authorized to eject from the Gold-and-Blue any juveniles who create trouble."

"Talbot doesn't create trouble," I objected as Talbot's face burned. "You aren't a very good judge of character, mister."

Beanstalk swung toward me, so I bolted down the corridor to Madge's and my compartment. And goggled. Gold armchairs, tucked against a midnight blue wall edged with gold trim, faced a huge picture window.

"Hi, Di," Pantelli called from his and Talbot's compartment across the passageway. They'd pulled out their mattress from the wall and were testing it for use as a trampoline.

"Ow!" Talbot banged his head on the ceiling. "Now I understand why gymnasts are short," he said ruefully. "Hey, guys, want to play Monopoly?"

"Never mind Monopoly," Pantelli replied and pulled a forest-patterned box from his duffel bag. Beaming, he held it up. "How 'bout a game of Treevial Pursuit?"

"Um...I think I'll check on Mrs. Chewbley," I said. Humming "Black Socks," I trotted down the passageway. Their voices floated after me.

"Thanks, Pantelli, but I'd rather sit and admire the scenery."

"Talbot, *we're still in the station*."

Clackety-clack! Mrs. Chewbley's knitting needles swooped and dove.

"Knitting soothes me," she explained cheerily as I shoved aside the chocolate creams and romance novels she'd dumped harum-scarum on the other armchair. "Goodness, that assistant head conductor was so *very* bad tempered. My, my!" The piano teacher wagged her head, dropping at least one hairpin onto her shoulder.

I surveyed Mrs. Chewbley's clothes, including the red flannel nightgown, which a good percentage of the train passengers had viewed earlier on the platform. Privately I agreed with Madge. Mrs. Chewbley was far too disorganized to be a chaperone. She sure was fun, though.

I was about to hint that a chocolate cream would be nice about now when a piercing whistle shrilled, followed by a snappish "All aboard, if it's not asking too much!" in Beanstalk's aggrieved tones. Suddenly the Gold-and-Blue was gliding from the station.

Now that we were actually leaving, I had an achy yearning for one of Mother's tearful hugs. Soon there'd be miles between us! I couldn't even do math that high.

I shoved open Mrs. Chewbley's window and peered up and down the platform. The Gold-and-Blue's gleaming cars stretched on either side of me: three locomotives, one baggage car, three coaches, two observation cars with panoramic glass domes, eleven sleeper cars like this one, and the rounded, mostly window, lounge car at the rear, for relaxing in and watching the miles slide away.

"Mother!" I yelled. An ocean of people waved back. I got dizzy peering among them. Where was Mother? It was like a *Where's Waldo?* scene. Only I'd never single her out. I didn't have time.

I did, however, have volume. "Mother!" I belted out. "MOTHER!"

"Dinah!" She pushed out of the crowd and blew kisses at me. Jack grinned and gave me the thumbs-up.

I waved vigorously at both of them. Heck, I'd miss Jack so much I wasn't even suspicious of him.

Well, not for now, anyway.

The train slid farther out of the station. Mother's red-and-white-checked dress shrank to a pinkish blot. I started to withdraw from the window.

Started to—and then I saw him.

Bowl Cut.

He was pelting alongside the train, hands fisted, cheeks fiercely puffing in and out, straight bowl-cut locks flapping around his head.

He stretched out a hand, grabbed a door handle and swung himself *splat*! against the train. Forcing the door open, he jammed himself and a plaid knapsack through.

Chapter Nine

The Elusive King: Elvis? An Elk?

The next morning, the Gold-and-Blue wound through the icy slopes of the Rockies. In the bright sun, their peaks burned a blinding white against the pure blue sky. We craned our necks to see the view out the dining car window.

"To the artist Yves Klein, blue was the color of infinity," Madge mused dreamily.

Just then a waiter presented us with breakfast, and Mrs. Chewbley, Pantelli, Talbot and I were more interested in tucking back fluffy scones, swirled butter and raspberry jam than hearing about art.

Madge dipped a fork into her own breakfast, if you could call it that: grapefruit and melon wedges. "I might do a whole canvas in blue someday," she said. "I've never done abstracts before, never wanted to, till now, seeing the Rocky Mountain sky..."

"There's a song in that somewhere," Talbot said. With the prongs of his fork, he carved a treble clef and bars into the crisp, thick navy of the tablecloth. And then some quarter notes. "Under a Rocky Mountain sky, I bid my darlin' good-bye," he sang softly.

Pantelli smothered a scone in jam. "But why would you bid your darlin' good-bye?" he asked, ever the analytical scientist, before cramming the scone in his mouth all at once.

"Yeah," Talbot conceded. "It's a sappy lyric. Besides, if I liked someone that much, I wouldn't bid her good-bye."

He glanced at me. Madge noticed and gave me yet another of her knowing, older-sisterly smiles. So *annoying*. I changed the subject.

"I questioned Beanstalk and the other conductors this morning," I announced. "They swear up and down that they haven't seen a bowl-cut passenger aboard."

Madge shook her head at me. "I'm relieved to hear that, Dinah. But I wish you wouldn't go around *grilling* train staff. It's so uncouth."

Talbot and Pantelli traded grimaces. Translation: Brace yourself for another Galloway sister spat.

The know-it-alls.

"Sorry to have embarrassed you by grilling the staff," I told Madge, who set down her grapefruit spoon and viewed me with astonishment.

Stunned silence all round. "Maybe this is an alien disguised as Dinah," Pantelli choked.

"Yeah, like in *Invasion of the Body Snatchers*," nodded Talbot. He sounded genuinely frightened.

I took advantage of Talbot and Pantelli's statue-like stares to steal extra scones from their plates. Madge was being statue-like as well, but needless to say I left *her* plate alone.

Out the window, I watched a doe and her white-speckled fawn snack on bluebells sprouting out of the snow. Had I just imagined that Bowl Cut actually made it through the train doors?

After breakfast we headed along to the games and library car. It had rows of booths whose tabletops were imprinted with chessboards. There was also a rack of books you could borrow.

Madge settled into a plush gold seat to sketch the mountains that were flowing past like endless vanilla sundaes. Pantelli produced Treevial Pursuit, at which Talbot and I quickly suggested climbing the stairs to the observation dome.

The domed ceiling and windows curved round us, giving us a three-hundred-sixty-degree view of the mountains. Also giving us the impression we were hurtling through the air, with no train around us. Pantelli made four pre-barfing noises. A four-barfer: wow. That proved it. The dome was better than the Sears Tower in Vancouver.

It occurred to me that I should suggest Pantelli exit the observation dome, but then the train angled down a steep hill and I forgot. Squashing my face against the front bubble window, I felt like an eagle, soaring past the snowy peaks, over the scarlet wildflowery slopes.

We plunged down an even steeper slope. "Way cool," Talbot exclaimed. He was doing the same squashed-face routine against the glass. He stretched out his arms and made *vroom!* noises followed by spluttering ones. "We're planes with engine trouble. Whoa, we're falling straight down the mountaaaiiiinnn...!"

"Ker-ash!" I shouted. I removed my sweater and tossed it on a nearby seat, the better to free up my arms for enjoying the plane-in-peril experience.

"BLEECCHH."

Pantelli was barfing into the lid of his Treevial Pursuit box. "I knew coming up to the observation dome was a mistake," he said glumly.

A rubbery, stem-like forefinger zoomed toward Pantelli's face. "*You* are a mistake," Beanstalk informed him, in a tone dripping with icicles.

All three of us jumped. Beanstalk sure moved stealthily, like some sort of mobile elastic band.

Sniffing, the conductor surveyed Talbot and me with equal scorn. "Plane trouble, indeed. More like *brain* trouble."

Beanstalk ordered everyone out of the observation dome. "Evacuate!" he commanded pompously. "Cleaning crew!" he called down the stairs.

"But I aimed and shot squarely in here," Pantelli

objected, showing Beanstalk the box lid and its, er, contents.

Back in the games car, we jammed into the booth with Madge and jabbered about Beanstalk's unreasonableness. "A tiny barfing incident," I complained.

Talbot, grimacing down at the lid Pantelli was holding out, said, "Maybe it's time to get rid of that. I'm not sure we need forensic evidence."

Madge was occupied in staring at her laptop, which she'd plugged into an Internet outlet. "No messages from Jack," she said mournfully, as Pantelli trotted off to drop the box lid in a garbage can. "I can't understand it. I mean, we've now been apart for seventeen hours and twenty-three minutes. This isn't like Jack."

Talbot, Pantelli and I shrugged at each other. These lovebirds were a whole different breed. "Repeatedly clicking *Get Mail* won't help," I advised Madge.

"Tons of messages from Mother and Geneva Rinaldi, though." Madge clicked on one. "They've appointed eight new bridesmaids. Here's what Geneva says: 'Matilda French of Charlottetown insists on lime green bridesmaids' dresses, the better to show off her new, Emerald City-themed arm tattoos.'"

With a sigh, my sister took up her sketchpad again. I slid her laptop in front of me to check my own e-mail. Specifically for an update from Mother about Ardle.

He's too weak to do more than mumble, but his

color's improved, she'd written. *The doctors are hopeful.*

I bashed out a message to Mother with questions to ask Ardle. *Make him tell you who the king is,* I wrote. *And no, I don't want to explain what I'm talking about.*

Talbot and Pantelli had got chess pieces from a steward and were already jockeying pawns and knights on the chessboard tabletop. "Wanna play?" Talbot invited. "You and I could take on Pantelli, master chess player of Lord Bithersby elementary."

"No, that's okay," I said. Chess, I thought. That involves a type of king. But Ardle could have been referring to almost anything. Chess king, card king—even Alaska king crab. Maybe Ardle was chasing a valuable recipe!

But there was no chess piece, card or recipe in the envelope, I reminded myself. Which brought us back to the elk stamp. Was the elk possibly considered the king of the Canadian north?

Right, Dinah. The *elk.*

Still, you never could be sure. I Googled "elk" and "stamp."

Did you mean the Elvis Presley Commemorative Stamp? Google asked helpfully.

"I have no idea," I replied out loud in a cross voice. Elvis: another king I hadn't thought of.

Talbot and Pantelli, engrossed in their game, didn't hear. Madge, doodling wildflowers in her sketchbook, cast me a brief sad-eyed glance. She had the Jack blues. Noticing that I'd typed "elk," she began drawing one. A sad-eyed one. Obviously if Madge had to feel lovelorn, so did the animal kingdom.

Thoughtfully, I drummed the sides of the laptop to the beat of "Black Socks." Couldn't figure out who or what the eighty-thousand-dollar king was, but a blazingly bright idea was occurring to me about what I could do for Madge. A Good Samaritan act, you might say.

I called up Gmail. *Jack.French@gmail.com*, I typed in.

I knew my future brother-in-law's password, not through any sneaky means, but because Jack himself had given it to me. Earlier in the summer, Mother had banned me from using my own e-mail address, juniorsleuth@gmail.com. Too many complaints from neighbors about the helpful hints I'd been sending on theft and fire prevention, recycling dos and don'ts, emotional health and well-being—you name it, I'd probably covered it.

One day, when I was hanging out at the Spotted Owl Advocacy Committee office, I'd informed Jack that I was in utter agony from e-mail deprivation. I had, I absolutely *had*, to let Talbot and Pantelli know I'd found the newest Deathstalkers comic at our favorite store, Komix R Us.

"You could phone Talbot and Pantelli," Jack suggested.

"Phone?! Please. That's so-o-o-o last century."

Jack, busy photocopying some rally notices, told me to use his e-mail. "My password's 'Madge,'" he flung over his shoulder.

Madge. How drearily predictable for a lovebird, I

thought at the time and again now, typing it in on the Gold-and-Blue.

My plan? A sickly sweet love message from Jack to Madge. Just the ticket to cheer Madge up, I decided.

Hmmm. Treacly. I wasn't really into that. But wait, there was that Elton John love song. I could borrow liberally from that:

I hope you don't mind that I put down in words
How wonderful life is while you're in the world.

Pretty sickening. Yup, Madge would love that.

Quoted adoringly for my true love, Madge Galloway, by her heart's desire, Jack French, I finished off and pressed *Send*.

I then took a minute to scan Jack's in-box. Curiosity was healthy, in my view. A true sign of an optimist, eager to find out what's around life's next corner.

I recognized all the sender names: mostly Madge, and Jack's colleagues on the Spotted Owl Advocacy Committee. I was preparing to exit when my gaze fell on a non-colleague name.

Veronica LaFlamme.

LaFlamme, I thought. The person who'd prevented Jack from coming to see Madge the other day.

The subject line beside Veronica's name read *Tried calling you today, but...*

I never could resist a *but*. Pushing aside what shreds of conscience I had about trespassing, I clicked on the message.

...some kidlet answered. I remembered your warning about an inquisitive redhead, so I hung up. I didn't want her to alert Madge to my existence.

I glared at the screen. Veronica LaFlamme was Peanut-Butter Voice! I *knew* that was a voice not to be trusted.

With growing horror, I read on.

I understand that you'd want to keep things between us a secret until you break the news to Madge.

Just as I'd feared. Jack was two-timing Madge!

Now that I had confirmation, I almost couldn't believe it. I sat and stewed, muttering out plans to draw and quarter Jack, among other slow-death punishments, until Madge glanced up from her elk sketch. "Why the scowl, Dinah?"

"I...um..." I could hardly admit to my sister that I'd been snooping in her fiancé's e-mail. However, I might as well start conditioning her to the single life right now.

"Emily Carr," I blurted. "Now there's an artist who never married, never had kids. She threw herself body and soul into her work."

"I suppose." Madge regarded me doubtfully.

"Ith not body and thoul I'm worried about. Ith teeth," announced a somewhat indistinct voice.

The salt-and-pepper-haired woman from the Pacific Central Station platform hovered over us. Her lips were pressed inward, covering her gums. "Loth my denturth," she explained, and her sorrowful gaze slid to Pantelli. "I thought maybe you could help?"

"I'm a dendrologist. Into bark, not enamel," Pantelli said crossly.

"Ah. Bark. A new, natural approach to denturth, I thuppoth." The woman shrugged. "Oh, well. I do have a thpare pair in the luggage car. Gueth thath where I'll have to go."

When she'd moved off, I leaned over to admire Madge's drawing. "Great elk there, Madge...ELK!" I exclaimed in sudden horror and jumped, knocking my knee against the table. "*Ow*. Excuse me, gotta zoom."

Madge, whose pencil-holding hand had been jarred by my abrupt exit, which had the effect of giving the elk an antenna, called acidly after me, "Maybe the reason Emily decided to stay single and childless was that *she'd spent time with a pre-teen*."

I charged up the observation dome stairs. The elk stamp! Dad's envelope, my only clue to the king mystery, was in the sweater I'd tossed on a seat.

On the stairs I brushed past two custodians, just finished cleaning, and did a mini high-jump over a pail full of suds they'd left at the top. The sweater had to be on the seat at the very front, where Talbot and I had done our witty out-of-control-plane routine.

My left arm was wrenched painfully back. What was this, rerun time? Same thing had happened under the big clock in Pacific Central Station.

I turned. A blanket descended on my head, the warm, snuggly kind I'd slept under last night. But this one was wrapped tightly around me, mummy style. Through its folds a very cold and unsnuggly voice whispered, "What have you done with the king?"

Chapter Ten

The Clues of the Fisherman

I was in a woolly fog. The gray blanket stuck on my glasses and filled my mouth. There was a bad joke in this somewhere, about all junior sleuths looking the same in the dark—i.e., totally helpless—but I was too frightened to make it.

In the middle of my fear, I knew one thing, though. I had to keep the whispering blanket-thrower from heading to that front seat, where my sweater lay in an untidy pile.

The Whisperer's shadow inked over me, making the blanket even darker. The Whisperer was too tall to be Bowl Cut, I thought suddenly.

I remembered reading somewhere that blind people instinctively sharpen their other senses to make up for the missing visual one. If I concentrated on sound and smell, I might be able to deduce something else about the Whisperer.

"So," I said conversationally, "what's new?"

My shoulder was freed from the clamp-like grip as the Whisperer loosened the blanket over my mouth. "C'mon, *give*. Where are you hiding it?"

"In the purser's safe, of course," I lied. Then, making my voice prim, I said, "After all, you can't trust anyone these days, don't you find?"

For which I got a shake. "You wanna stay healthy? It'd be just too bad if the *Tomorrow's Cool Talent* host had to say, 'Our next guest, Dinah Galloway, has a lateness problem. As in *permanent* lateness.'"

Hot as I was inside the blanket, I shivered. Another shake. I was starting to feel like a castanet. "Next time I pay you a visit, have the king ready," the Whisperer instructed, in such a hissy voice I couldn't tell if it belonged to a man or a woman. He, she or it then shoved me forward. Hard. I landed, blanketed face first, in the custodians' sudsy bucket.

I was just pulling the sopping blanket off my equally sopping head when footsteps tapped up behind me.

"I might have known," Beanstalk snapped. Curving over me in that rubbery way he had, the conductor twitched a disapproving forefinger. "You're not happy unless you're disrupting my day, are you? I suppose a budding star will do anything for attention. CLEANERS!" he shouted and began to bounce indignantly toward the stairs in pursuit of them.

"Wait!" Wringing out chunks of my hair, I slip-slid after him through the spilled suds. "You must've passed the person who—"

"Not another word," Beanstalk sniffed. He rolled a thunderous look down his sloping nose at me. Then he shrilled, "CLEANERS!" and sprinted down the stairs, three at a time.

Retrieving my sweater, I clumped down the stairs after him. With one hand I continued wringing out my hair; with the other I clutched the precious but puzzling envelope. Dad, I thought, what is the secret you left? Who is the king?

"Oh no, Dinah!" Madge wailed, setting down her elk sketch. "Not another water incident!"

I'd had quite a few of these in May, aboard the Alaska cruise ship *Empress Marie*. Let's just say the thief I was pursuing had kind of a one-track mind when it came to ways of trying to silence me.

I hesitated. Madge was already uneasy about my claim of seeing Bowl Cut force his way onto the train. If she found out about the whispering blanket-thrower, I'd probably find myself at the nearest airport, awaiting the next plane back to Vancouver.

"It's okay," I assured Madge. "A minor mishap."

Other Gold-and-Blue passengers were gaping at me over their books and chess games. All those faces, still and staring, like the moons of Saturn. One of them might just be feigning surprise. One of them might be the Whisperer.

I scanned the faces, back and forth, till I grew dizzy—and then, as abruptly as if it had collided with a roadblock, my gaze stopped. One person wasn't staring. One person was holding a tourist guidebook about Western Canada in front of her face.

I could see her chestnut hair, though. And her red dress.

Mrs. Zanatta!

What was she doing on the Gold-and-Blue?

"And where's her little boy?" I muttered.

Beanstalk breezed back, cleaners in tow. Hearing me, he whipped his rubbery neck round to follow my stare. "Ryan Zanatta is playing *quietly* in the Gold-and-Blue Day Camp," he informed me, adding snootily, "We like our adult patrons to enjoy themselves. To escape from children."

With a foul parting look at me, he and the cleaners paraded on.

Much *you* know, Beanstalk, I thought grimly. Ryan's playing quietly because, for whatever reason, he's the kid who doesn't speak.

I glanced at Mrs. Zanatta again. Granted, in a short while we'd be in Jasper, the first of two stops the Gold-and-Blue would be making so passengers could take side trips. The next stop would be Winnipeg.

Maybe Mrs. Zanatta really was brushing up on her landmarks.

But holding the guidebook upside down was an awfully strange way to read about them.

~~~

On the pale sand by Jasper's Annette Lake, out of Madge's and Mrs. Chewbley's hearing range, I filled my fellow junior sleuths in about the Whisperer.

"That does it," Talbot said. From his knapsack, he withdrew two clunky, wire-sprouting black rectangles. Er, walkie-talkies. "Keep this with you at all times," he instructed, handing one to me.

I fought back a howl of protest that would have echoed across Annette Lake to the distant blue Mount Edith Cavell, with its splotch of snow at the peak.

Talbot, Pantelli, Madge, Mrs. Chewbley and I had spread out blankets to enjoy the gi-normous sandwiches the Gold-and-Blue chef had provided. There were an awful lot of them: egg salad, smoked salmon and cream cheese, tuna, blackened chicken, and my favorite, banana-peanut-butter-and-honey. Plus garlicky pickles, Caesar salad, potato salad—we couldn't gobble fast enough.

It turned out Mrs. Chewbley had ordered for ten. "You never know how hungry you'll get," she'd giggled. There were so many sandwiches she'd had to stuff some of them in her flowered-print bag.

I'd sort of hoped Talbot would forget about bringing along the walkie-talkies. He'd constructed them last month out of old telephones and radio transmitters. Oh, and elastic bands and duct tape for holding everything together were also an integral part of the design. The walkie-talkies were Talbot's solution to my habit of running into villains—and sometimes not running away fast enough.

Pantelli burst into rude laughter at the sight of the walkie-talkies. I clapped a hand over his mouth. After all, Talbot meant well.

"Fine. I'll carry this thing around," I promised, though not in the most gracious tone. Talbot was such a worrywart! I stuffed the walkie-talkie into my knitted rainbow purse, whose strap I'd refastened with safety pins. "At the very least, it'll build up my biceps."

This was a complaint as much as a joke, but Madge, emerging from the lake, overheard and smiled with approval. "It's great that you're giving thought to physical fitness," she remarked and proceeded to squeeze water from her auburn tresses. Why was it, I wondered, that when Madge did this she resembled Aphrodite fresh from the foam, as a reporter had remarked last month? Whereas I looked like I'd just been through the carwash—without the car.

"C'mon, Di," Talbot urged. Yelling, he and Pantelli charged into the lake with maximum splashes. I followed more reluctantly, expecting icy temperatures.

But Annette Lake was surprisingly warm. "The lake's shallow," Pantelli explained, treading water ahead of me. "Annette's a mere leftover of a way bigger lake that once covered this whole valley."

We swam easily to the raft anchored twenty-five yards out. Hauling myself up, I prepared to bask in the sun.

Pantelli challenged Talbot to a race to shore and back. "Go on," I told Talbot, who had a concerned, should-we really-leave-you? expression under the long, wet, but still soulful forelock he kept shoving out of his eyes. "Unless the *Jaws* shark shows up, I'll be fine."

Both boys made fins with their hands and hummed the DOO-doo-DOO-doo *Jaws* theme music. I laughed heartily. I believe that sophisticated wit should be encouraged.

Talbot and Pantelli kick-started themselves into violent crawls toward the shore.

I tilted my head back and closed my eyes. Maybe the sun would tan my freckles together. That'd be a better option than trying to scrub them off with a Brillo pad, which I'd done in the spring after Liesl the Weasel Dubuque made fun of them: *You oughtta write START on one side of your face and FINISH on the other, and challenge people to find their way through the freckle maze.*

Roars from the beach. Talbot had got there first and was pretending to storm it in a reenactment of D-Day, 1944, at the beaches of Normandy.

Talbot was a history buff. At home he had all these board games of famous battles: D-Day, Gettysburg, Waterloo, the Somme. He and his dad replayed the battles, complete with their own sound effects of bomb explosions, gunfire and people screaming with agony as they died.

Normally Talbot and his dad were such *quiet* people too...

Lately Talbot had started reading historical biographies. This meant his socials marks, already stratospheric, soared even higher. I'd overheard a teacher remark regretfully to him, "I just wish I could give you more than a hundred percent, Talbot."

Like, give me a break.

Right now, Madge, a lot less enthusiastic about his passion for history, was shooing Allied Commander St. John away. "Not yet!" I heard him shout. "I have to secure the beach first!"

I grinned. *Not yet, not yet*, I started to hum. I couldn't get "Black Socks" out of my head. It was as if the song was pestering me.

Nobody else on or near the raft. I might as well let 'er rip.

Black socks, they never get dirty,

The longer you wear them, the blacker they get.

The words echoed satisfyingly around Annette Lake. This was fun. When I sang, I didn't care about freckles or anything.

Someday I think I will wash them,

But something keeps telling me...

"You can do better songs than that."

I stopped in mid-note. As, a few seconds later, did my echo around Annette Lake. A man in a gray tracksuit was regarding me comfortably from a rowboat close to the raft. A fishing pole and metal tackle box lay in the boat. The man, who had a pointed beard, wore a gray tweed hat, gleaming all over with the lures and hooks stuck into it.

Based on my experience in the observation dome, I wasn't in the mood to welcome new acquaintances. Talbot and Pantelli, thrashing through the water again, were still far away. But the fisherman looked so harmless, almost sleepy, that the scream I'd considered volleying to shore limped out as an "Um..."

"I would've thought the old standards would be more your type of song," the fisherman said as, glasses-less, I squinted at him. "Cole Porter, say. Or Irving Berlin. Now there was a guy who knew how to write belter-outers. Why, in a few years I could see you playing Annie in *Annie Get Your Gun*."

My jaw did a slow amazed drop. Playing Annie—she's the rootin' tootin' cowgirl who gets to sing "There's No Business Like Show Business"—was a secret dream of mine. Annie was so like me: untidy and troublesome, but good-hearted in a wacky kind of way, and, of course, equipped with volume, *volume*, VOLUME.

"You're right," I said meekly. "I do know better songs. It's just that 'Black Socks' reminds me of something. Of a problem."

The fisherman trailed his paddles in the lake. The surface water skimmed silkily over them. "Of a king?"

Instantly suspicious, I scrambled up and stood at the opposite end of the raft from him.

"There are kings and kings," the fisherman said easily. By squinting fiercely, I could see that he was smiling. "Britain's Charles the Second, for example. Did you know that to escape his enemies, the Roundheads, he fled up an oak tree? They didn't notice him, and he was able to escape to

France. Very clever of Charles the Second, not to mention quite spry of him.

"A shame his dad, Charles the First, didn't take a—wait for it—*leaf* out of his book." The fisherman's shoulders heaved with merriment. "Charles the First, not a good hider at all, was easily captured by the Roundheads."

"Huh," I commented, wondering just how much time this guy had spent in the sun. I also wondered if it was time to start hollering. Maybe Bowl Cut and/or the Whisperer had sent him to pry information from me.

"Ah, yes, Charles the First," the fisherman went on, as if we had all day to muse about dead monarchs. "Handsome fellow. Not the brightest, though."

I would've frowned at the man except that I was already squinting. "Who *are* you?"

The fisherman winked. "Someone who hopes for an answer from you, Dinah Galloway. About where a king might be hidden. Not in a tree this time. Somewhere much harder to detect."

Talbot and Pantelli were chopping ever closer through the water. Growing bolder, I marched across the raft to glare at the fisherman. "I don't have any answers for you. None."

The fisherman smiled, his teeth showing very white against his pointy beard. "But you will. I'd bet on you anytime."

With comfortable backward strokes, he began rowing away. "Now just a minute," I called angrily. "You're being cryptic. I *hate* cryptic."

He was fast turning into a speck. "COME BACK HERE," I bellowed, stepping forward some more.

Memo to self: Next time you walk across a raft, keep in mind that you're nearsighted. My right foot met air...

SSPPLLAASSHH.

It was Talbot who grabbed me under the arms and hoisted me to the surface. "That was the most pathetic dive I've ever seen," he told me as I coughed out water. "Next time you enter the lake, use the *ladder*."

Chapter Eleven

The Lady Vanishes

Talbot, Pantelli and Madge were in the observation dome along with other passengers, watching Jasper shrink as we pulled away into the Rockies again. Sitting on my own in the dining car, I pressed my nose against the window and stared at the wide, sparkling Athabasca River flowing parallel to the railway tracks. Dad just couldn't have had the mysterious eighty-thousand-dollar king on him when he died, I decided. Or—now here was a gruesome possibility—what if he'd had the king in the envelope, but someone removed it from his body?

I rubbed my temples. Whenever I thought about possibilities, as opposed to facts, my head hurt. Hypotheticals, the *what-ifs* and *supposes* of life, didn't agree with me.

Beanstalk strode by and I asked him for a Coke. He immediately looked offended, but, seeing no waiters around, paced off with huge angry strides to fetch me one.

I closed my eyes. Ardle McBean rose up against the lids, displaying his nicotine-yellow teeth and asking for the king. "I don't have it," I muttered.

"Well, now you do," Beanstalk snapped. He plunked a glass of Coke on the table so that the ice clanked furiously. My walkie-talkie, which I'd set by the place mat, jumped. Beanstalk looked down his Rocky Mountain-slope nose at it. "Let me know if I should dispose of that scrap metal for you," he sniffed and swung off, slinging a blue napkin over his shoulder with a *slap!*

I glugged back a good portion of the Coke. The ice cubes crowded up to my nose, tickling it. Ah, the small pleasures of life.

Blurry through the ice cubes, a face appeared. A plump, worried one.

Edwina Chewbley's.

Her chin was trembling so badly her whole head shook. *Ping!* A hairpin popped out to land on some cutlery. Lifting a gold and blue napkin, the piano teacher mopped at her forehead. "I've been searching everywhere for you, Dinah. When I got back to the train, *I saw Bowl Cut getting on just ahead of me.*"

"Holy Toledo," I breathed.

"I followed him, or tried to," Mrs. Chewbley reported. "Amazing he didn't hear me. I was huffing and puffing behind him all the time." She gave an apologetic little laugh. "I suppose I really *should* cut down on my chocolate creams."

She began to fan herself with the napkin. "Someone got in the way, and Bowl Cut slipped out of view. I'm so sorry I doubted you. I've already left a note for the head conductor saying I must speak to him as soon as possible."

Mrs. Chewbley began to sway in her seat. "Goodness, all that rushing about...I'm not used to it...If only I had something to drink..."

Afraid she was about to faint, I jumped up and waved at Beanstalk, down at the other end of the dining car. Sniffing, he crooked a long forefinger in an annoyed, just-a-minute signal and continued punching keys on his BlackBerry.

I sat down again. "Some Coke?" I offered, pushing my glass toward Mrs. Chewbley.

Mrs. Chewbley surveyed the Coca-Cola, which had bits of squashed lemon floating about in it. Pounding lemon wedges into pulp with a spoon is one of my favorite sports. "Er...no. You drink it up, Dinah. I'd rather order a—"

The train let out a long whistle, the kind you hear at home from faraway that makes you long to run off and explore the world.

At the moment it was preventing me from hearing Mrs. Chewbley. "Pardon?" I shouted.

Mrs. Chewbley opened her mouth. The whistle sounded again, as if it were blasting from her lungs. We both laughed. Shrugging good-humoredly, Mrs. Chewbley picked up the saltshaker and emptied some out on the table. *L-E-M-* she began tracing in the salt—but then the whistle died out.

Oh, *lemonade.* I windmilled my arms at Beanstalk. I drank from my Coke and pointed at Mrs. Chewbley. Really, I should be in improv. But Beanstalk merely flapped an impatient wrist at me.

Mrs. Chewbley proceeded to cluck about Bowl Cut and how nasty he was to be giving little girls frights like this.

Just because I'm height-challenged doesn't mean I'm little, I thought—but I couldn't feel annoyed at Mrs. Chewbley. She'd out-detectived me by noticing Bowl Cut.

"Such shady goings-on," Mrs. Chewbley clucked. She started knitting again. *Click, click!*

Clucks and clicks. Even though I wanted to charge up and down the train, alerting everyone that Bowl Cut was aboard, I began to grow sleepy. It'd been a vigorous swim at Annette Lake, not to mention the fifty-odd sandwiches I'd packed away...

"Dreadful fellow," clucked Mrs. Chewbley.

Cluck, cluck...click, click...

Snap, snap! Twigs crunched as Charles the Second climbed down from the tree he'd been hiding in. "Do you think they'll find me?" he asked, brushing twigs off his black socks.

"I've been trying to find you myself," I replied. "I'm wondering if you're the king everyone's talking about."

Charles sniffed. "Well, I ought to be."

I held out Dad's unmailed letter to him. The scrawled return address gave a wriggle. It changed from my home address to a face that promptly stuck its tongue out at us.

"Very rude, and to a royal, no less," Charles remarked disapprovingly over his pointed beard.

"You rather look like the fisherman on Annette Lake," I told him.

"A fisher— ? How dare you? Guards!" shouted Charles, brushing leaves off a satin sleeve.

None came. "Those bloody Roundheads," the King fumed. "I suppose they'll be here any minute." He tugged at his beard. "Hmm. You can't think of a cleverer hiding place than a tree, can you? Being such an imposing figure, I do tend to stand out. What a bother! And you haven't been any help at all," he accused.

"But I wanted you to help me."

"Impertinence!" Charles scrambled up the tree again, and I got another flash of black socks. They didn't go very well with his satiny, lace-trimmed outfit.

"Isn't it about time you bolted to France?" I suggested helpfully. "Wait … "

"Wait," I mumbled and woke myself up. "Hey, Mrs. Chewbley, you won't believe the dream I just—"

"Mrs. *Who*-bley?" inquired the woman sitting across the table from me.

And, with a sick feeling, I saw it wasn't Mrs. Chewbley at all, but Mrs. Zanatta.

Chapter Twelve

Di-verging from Reality

Nobody had seen Mrs. Chewbley.

What was worse, Beanstalk flapped a note in my face that was signed *Edwina Chewbley*. It said she'd decided to stay in Jasper for a few extra days and not take the train any farther.

"That's forged," I said flatly. I glared at Mrs. Zanatta. "You're in this king thing, aren't you? *What did you do with her?*"

Mrs. Zanatta was as scarlet as her dress. "I'd hoped for a confidential word with you, Miss Galloway—though up to now on this trip, after the butter-tart incident, I've been hiding from you."

To our fast-gathering onlookers, she added, "Honestly, Miss Galloway was alone when I arrived," and edged away.

Head Conductor Wiggins, a tall, gray-haired man whose gold buttons blinked and winked at me from his navy uniform, stepped forward. "I escorted Mrs. Chewbley onto the platform at Jasper myself—she needed help, as her bag had split open somehow."

Beanstalk, standing nearby, flushed angrily at this reminder of his little adventure with the piano teacher at the journey's start. "You see? The Chewbley dame had her bag with her. There is no question of her being aboard."

"Mrs. Chewbley took her bag because she'd crammed extra sandwiches into it," I argued.

The head conductor glanced at Madge, Talbot and Pantelli, who were all gaping at me. His lean, handsome features were doubtful. "Miss Galloway, you say Mrs. Chewbley wanted to warn you about a man with a bowl cut?"

I brightened. "Yeah, did you get her note?"

Head Conductor Wiggins turned to Beanstalk. "Did you see any note?"

Beanstalk snorted. His goggly gaze wandered to Madge, where it stuck. A silly grin simpered across his long face. "May I offer you an iced tea, Miss Galloway? This," he flicked his bulbous eyes at me, "must be very upsetting for you."

I could tell Madge was not overly pleased with me. *Just once*, her lupine-blue eyes blazed, *just once I'd like to enjoy a peaceful vacation!*

With some difficulty, her sisterly loyalty triumphed. "Dinah isn't upsetting at all," she fibbed coldly.

Beanstalk visibly withered, his shoulders sagging and his rubbery frame bending into an unhappy C.

"You had to have seen Mrs. Chewbley," I accused. "Remember how I was waving and waving at you?"

"The young lady could be mentally ill," interrupted a tall, thin, sour-faced woman in a nurse's uniform. She muscled forward, treading on Pantelli's foot so that he yelped in pain. She brandished a black medical bag that read, in severe gothic letters, BEVERLY BALLANTYNE, RN. "I'm in charge of the train infirmary."

"But are you *trained*," Pantelli wisecracked, massaging his foot.

I knew he was being silly in an effort to cheer me up. But Nurse Ballantyne scowled and sharply rapped her bag as if she rather wished it were Pantelli's head.

Nurse Ballantyne had a very nasal voice. She gave the impression there was a bad smell she was trying to force out of her nostrils all the time she spoke. Now the nurse placed a palm on my forehead. "I understand you're set to appear on *Tomorrow's Cool Talent*."

I glared at her. "*A passenger has vanished*."

Ignoring me, Nurse Ballantyne pronounced, "Stage fright. Nerves." She cracked open her bag with a snap and reached for a syringe with a large needle.

"There's no need for that," Madge protested, and Talbot moved between the nurse and me.

Head Conductor Wiggins asked wearily, "Miss Galloway, you haven't *really* seen Mrs. Chewbley since our departure from Jasper, have you?"

Beanstalk shot his neck out of his conductor uniform collar and glared at me. "You dreamed the whole thing. I saw you. You were *napping*."

"Mrs. Chewbley is on the train," I said stubbornly. I'm good at stubborn. "She warned me about Bowl Cut."

The Gold-and Blue whipped past a meadow, reddish gold in the setting sun. From some other window, Mrs. Chewbley might be watching it. Might be unable to speak if she'd been removed against her will.

Yet no one believed me. Even Madge, Talbot and Pantelli were looking at me questioningly.

Could I have dreamt it?

My eyes dropped to the *L-E-M* the piano teacher had traced in the salt.

"She *was* here!" I exclaimed, pointing. "See where she—"

"I think it's time to stop this nonsense at once," Nurse Ballantyne announced, slamming her bag down on the table.

And the salt jiggled, erasing the *L-E-M*.

Sighing, Head Conductor Wiggins ordered a search of the train. From the rigid set of his jaw, I knew he wasn't pleased. But I had to give him credit. Someone had reported a vanishing passenger, and he was going to investigate, even if that someone was an untidy pre-teen with attitude.

"I appreciate what you're doing, but I can tell your enthusiasm quotient is low," I told him.

Madge bustled me back to our compartment, though not before I glimpsed Mrs. Zanatta's red dress flashing into a compartment two doors down.

Click! Madge shut our door. She said gently, "You were asleep when Mrs. Chewbley disappeared. Isn't it possible you *did* dream that she was back on the train?"

"No." I pulled my hand away. "She saw Bowl Cut and decided to warn me."

"But why would this Bowl Cut person be on the train?"

"Ummm..." I didn't want to explain to Madge about having Dad's envelope.

Madge pushed back her auburn hair into a ponytail and let it drop again. "Sometimes Mother and I—and Jack too—notice that your imagination tends to be—well, vivid. It's, um, all part of your natural energy, I guess. Which tends to be—well, excessive," she said.

All this hesitating was—well, grating on my nerves. "Do you want to chat when you've come up with a final draft?" I invited.

To my surprise, this rude remark made her grin. "You're a bright girl, Dinah. What you do with your singing is incredible. Like Pablo Casals with his cello. Or Venus Williams with her tennis game. Bright people, especially when they're young, can be overly sensitive. Do you," she stopped, and then got it out all in a rush, "ever think that you see Dad?"

I goggled at her. Wow, these older siblings were frighteningly observant. I'd thought no one knew.

"I...um..."

To me, Dad's appearances were quite normal. I mean, it was simple. Either, A, he was there or, B, he was a figment of my imagination.

"It's just that..." Madge absently twisted the pinned-on strap of my rainbow purse. "If you're imagining Dad, then maybe you imagined Mrs. Chewbley."

Chapter Thirteen

The Boy Who Wouldn't Talk

No one believed me, and now my sister thought I chatted with ghosts. Well, I did: one ghost, at any rate. And why *shouldn't* a girl have a variety of friends? At school they were always telling us to believe in diversity.

Feeling very sorry for myself, I did what any junior sleuth would do. I turned my attention to a loose end.

"A loose end," Pantelli repeated as I rapped on Mrs. Zanatta's door. "Is that like a dangling modifier?"

"Don't be daft," I said—unfortunately, just as Mrs. Zanatta swung her compartment door open.

She cut me off before I could explain that I didn't find *her* daft, just sinister. "Dinah, you've made it clear you want nothing to do with me. So I'm not going to try approaching you again. It was Ardle's idea. We met in the park, and I told him about Ryan and how we were taking the train to

Toronto. Ardle said you would be on the Gold-and-Blue too, and he thought you might—well, never mind." Mrs. Zanatta sighed. "I'm sorry to have troubled you."

Behind her, cross-legged on the floor, Ryan was clamping Lego pieces together. Red, yellow and blue pieces swooped and blurred through the air as he blended them into a castle. Wow. I had never got beyond the single-square-room stage.

"The new Christopher Wren," Talbot congratulated Ryan. "Christopher Wren, the great English architect who rebuilt London after the Great Fire of 1666, started out playing with blocks, just like Ryan. Actually, he played them with the future King Charles the Second," he explained.

When Charles wasn't practicing climbing trees, I thought. Switching my gaze back from Ryan to his mom, I demanded, "Ardle suggested you approach me? And *not* about the king?"

"You must be quite the monarchist," Mrs. Zanatta said, puzzled. "Always thinking about kings! In any case, Ardle was trying to help Ryan. You see, Ryan has a stutter. In kindergarten, kids made fun of him, and he stopped speaking. Even older kids like that horrible Liesl Dubuque give him a hard time."

Mentally I handed a pink slip to my distrust of Mrs. Zanatta. Anyone who referred to Liesl as horrible couldn't be all bad.

Mrs. Zanatta stooped to hug her son. "You don't like it when I talk about you, do you, honey? I'm sorry."

She smiled up at me. "*But Ryan can sing perfectly*. It's incredible. Ardle thought you might be willing to sing with him, you know, to bring him out of his shell a bit. He's so shy about his stutter."

I was feeling about the size of one of Ryan's Lego pieces. No wonder Mrs. Zanatta thought I'd be unsympathetic. As well as hurling a butter tart at her, I'd accused her of co-kidnapping Mrs. Chewbley!

"Ryan and I have some singing to do," I announced.

Mrs. Zanatta, Talbot and Pantelli left the two of us to belt out "On Top of Old Smoky," "This Old Man," and other kidlet faves to music from a CD. I also taught Ryan "Black Socks." "If I'm stuck with it in my brain, so should you be," I informed him.

Ryan's voice was pitch-divine and sweet, like a choirboy's. But he wouldn't say anything to me, even after I told him that, in my view, a lot of people who could speak without stuttering were the ones who should keep quiet. Even after I made him laugh with stories about the evil hair-cutting prank I'd played on Liesl, and her egg retaliation. (Weird—I was furious at Liesl, but when I talked about our feud, it was all quite funny.)

Ryan just wouldn't speak. One day, I vowed, I would figure out a way to encourage him to.

Later, while Talbot played ping-pong against Pantelli and Ryan, Mrs. Zanatta and I went for pizza in the dining car. Because I was curious—my normal state, in other words—Ryan's mom gave me the Cliff's Notes briefing about stuttering.

About one percent of the population, and four times as many males as females, stutter. There can be different reasons for stuttering, such as the brain processing language in a different way. Often stuttering runs in the family; Mrs. Zanatta's grandfather had stuttered.

"I'm taking Ryan to Toronto to see a world-famous speech specialist," she finished, peeling her first piece of pizza from the box. Up to then, Mrs. Zanatta had been too busy talking to eat. She had a proud, shiny-eyed expression as she described how Ryan's creativity far outpaced his problem, if only he'd realize that.

"I'm hoping the specialist will teach Ryan some exercises to practice speaking—and to build up his confidence." Mrs. Zanatta's eyes grew shinier, and I saw she had tears in them.

Chapter Fourteen

A Patient Is Smuggled Off

Ryan...Mrs. Chewbley...my thoughts spun like an out-of-control Ferris wheel, and I couldn't sleep.

I pulled the laptop toward me and logged on to Jack's e-mail. I'd intended to write Mother, but there, in front of me, like a malevolent toad, sat a new message from Veronica LaFlamme.

Jack,

You're my ideal man, but I can't wait forever. Isn't it better to tell Madge now? Trust me, speaking as a gal myself, it's better to be honest.

I'm just so glad you agreed to meet me at J.J. Bean's café. That secluded nook you chose was perfect.

J.J. Bean's! That was *Madge* and Jack's favorite place. They met there for breakfast and had long, meaningful talks over steaming coffee and fat fruit muffins.

Some guys in your situation would've refused to have anything to do with me. Thank goodness you're so open-minded!

Vee

I made indignant exploding noises that half-woke Madge. "You having a nightmare, Di?" Her hand flailed sleepily to give me a reassuring pat.

It's *your* nightmare, I reflected grimly. Little do you know you're not a fiancée anymore, but an old Flamme.

So "Vee" was glad Jack was "open-minded" about meeting other women! I punched *Reply*. In a return message to Veronica LaFlamme, I bashed out, *Why "Vee," by the way? Get it—y...v...? Gosh, I'm a fun guy. And y'know the reason I agreed to meet you? Huh?*

I thought of yet another king and smiled evilly. *You remind me of my favorite movie star. Yes—KING KONG!!! Oh, and try not to forget the deodorant next time, okay?—Jack.*

I pressed *Send* and felt extremely satisfied. Next time, a mega-insulting group-send message to Jack's entire contacts list.

"Fish!" I announced.

Talbot, Pantelli and I were playing cards in the games room. None of us could sleep.

"Poor Mrs. Chewbley," Pantelli mourned. "Nicest piano teacher I ever had. With her gone, I guess it's back to mean Mrs. Grimsbottom."

"Mrs. Chewbley isn't dead," I scolded. "At least, I *hope*..." I couldn't finish the sentence.

"Maybe she's dotty and wandered off," Talbot suggested. "My grandfather did that once. Gran phoned the police, who searched everywhere—and then Grandfather calmly strolled in the door. He'd spent the weekend in Vegas. 'Didn't I tell you?' he asked Gran. Now he wears one of those tracking bracelets for his safety—and for *their* bank account, Gran says. She's still steamed because Grandfather gambled away five grand at the Seven Kings Hotel in Vegas."

Pantelli laughed, but I was staring thoughtfully at Talbot. "Kings," I repeated. "You're our resident history expert. Tell me about Charles the First."

Talbot made a chopping motion with his hand. "Lost his head, Di. The Roundheads axed it off."

"Cool," breathed Pantelli—but I was hearing Ardle's feeble parting words as the stretcher attendants bore him off.

A king who lost his head.

"The eighty-thousand-dollar king Dad was keeping for Ardle," I breathed. "It's something to do with Charles the First!"

"Hail the junior sleuth," Talbot said, grinning. "But, Sherlock, of what nature is this valuable? A painting? Naw, that wouldn't fit in an envelope. A coin or letter, maybe?"

"A stamp," Pantelli suggested.

I produced the envelope, held it upside down and shook it. "Whatever it was, it's long gone," I sighed.

Still, I couldn't get Charles the First out of my mind. "So who were the Roundheads, and why were they after him?" I asked Talbot.

Talbot got the solemn academic look he so often wore at school. "The Roundheads were people who believed in the power of parliament, of elected representation. As opposed to Charles and his supporters, the Cavaliers, who believed that the king should be all-powerful.

"The Roundheads were so-called because they cut their hair short to distinguish themselves from the Cavaliers, who had long curly manes. That part of it was pretty childish."

I thought of my feud with Liesl, which, as Madge had pointed out, centered on hair. "Yeah," I agreed sheepishly.

"Well, the Roundheads put Charles on trial and beheaded him in 1649. Two years later, there was this tremendous battle at Worcester," Talbot's dark eyes were really sparkling now, "where the Roundheads totally trounced the Cavaliers. Here, I'll show you," and Talbot began moving the playing cards around on the tablecloth.

Pantelli was studying the envelope under the booth lamp. "Hey, Tal, put the troop movements on hold for a minute." He pointed to Dad's messy handwriting. "Look at this!"

I shrugged. "Welcome to a new concept, Pantelli. The return address."

"No, *look*."

I looked. "A postal code—wait, no, it isn't!" I exclaimed. "It's a phone number—*and not ours*."

I was back in my compartment, trying once more to sleep. But the phone number from the envelope danced in my head. Two-five-five-nine-nine-five-five. Did it belong to someone Dad had given the king to? Or who at least knew something about what and where the king was?

Reluctantly, Talbot, Pantelli and I had nixed the idea of phoning the number. It was too late, even by Vancouver time. I'd have to wait—the activity I hated most—till the morning to call.

Taunting me, the numbers did cartwheels. I sat up, not bothering to try to sleep anymore. So much for the soothing lull of a moving train.

Just a minute. There was no lulling movement. The Gold-and-Blue was still.

Leaning over my sleeping sister, I pushed the curtain aside to peer out the window.

We were at a station. Weird—I thought our next stop was in the morning, in Winnipeg. It was 1:30 AM and inky black outside.

Except for that splash of lights over to the right. I grabbed my housecoat and padded out into the passageway in my fluffy white cat-face slippers (a gift from Wilfred last Christmas).

"Good evening, Miss Galloway."

It was a conductor, but a nice freckle-faced one, not the rubbery, disapproving Beanstalk. "Freddy McClusky, at your service," he said. "I enjoyed your performance in *The Moonstone* last year. Man, what a set of pipes! With that and your red hair, you're a miniature Bette Midler."

The Bette Midler part I was pleased about; the miniature, less so. "Why are we stopping? An emergency?"

"A routine." Freddy grinned. "We always stop the Gold-and-Blue at Saskatoon, or just outside it, actually, at one thirty in the morning. Just for half an hour to drop off or pick up packages." He wrinkled his nose good-naturedly. "Too bad. I have an aunt here who makes the best Saskatoon berry pie. But there's no time to visit her. That'd be the one advantage of being the new guy stuck on the nightshift, but no-o-o."

He started describing his aunt's recipe, which called for cramming in as many of the juicy dark berries as possible.

But for once I wasn't in the mood to think about food. Nurse Ballantyne was shoving past us, her crisp white uniform crackling with static. "Make way. Patient leaving. Make way," she ordered, sounding even more nasal than usual. Her bony hands shot out and—*wompf!*—flattened Freddy against one wall, me against the other.

Behind her, two ambulance attendants carried a body on a stretcher. The body was covered by a blanket, and the head was completely wrapped in bandages.

The train stopped to drop off packages, Freddy had said.

And sometimes people, it seemed.

I stared hard at the patient, momentarily halted between the two stretcher bearers. Nurse Ballantyne was wrenching at the exit doors.

"Who's under the bandages?" I demanded.

"A frail passenger with a head injury," the nurse snapped. "I'll thank you not to slow us down. Getting my patient to the hospital is vital in a case like this."

"In a case like what?" Jogging up beside the stretcher, I poked a finger in the patient's tummy. "This patient's awfully well-fed for being frail." Chewbley well-fed, I was thinking. What better way of sneaking the piano teacher off the train than wrapped up in bandages?

Nurse Ballantyne held the door open for the stretcher bearers. The first backed gingerly out, trying to keep the stretcher straight. Nevertheless, it tipped slightly, and the patient started a headfirst slide.

"Be careful," I said and scowled at Nurse Ballantyne. "That's Edwina Chewbley, isn't it? You kidnapped her because she knows too much."

Nurse Ballantyne's right hand flared out from under her cloak. This time I was *wompf!*-ed against the wall and held there. The nurse's beady eyes were two tiny black cannonballs. "Don't cross me, Dinah Galloway," she whispered.

I squirmed, feeling like a bug being pinned to a Bristol board for a science project. "That telltale whisper," I retorted. "You're the one who threw the blanket over me in the observation car."

The two tiny black cannonballs gleamed for a second. Then Nurse Ballantyne released me so abruptly I crumpled to the floor. She strode off the train, her white-stockinged legs flashing under the station lamps.

Nurse Ballantyne might have finished with me. I wasn't done with her yet. Not as long as I had VOLUME.

"HELP! HELP! NURSE BALLANTYNE'S SMUGGLING MRS. CHEWBLEY OFF THE TRAIN!"

Heads began popping out of sleeping compartments. On the platform, porters stopped loading their dollies with packages. The stretcher carriers paused too, with doubtful glances at Nurse Ballantyne.

In the awkward silence, Freddy murmured admiringly, "What a voice, Miss Galloway. I just wish we had a brass section."

Nurse Ballantyne began cracking her bony knuckles. The *snaps*! echoed out into the still darkness around the station. "Proceed on with the patient! An ambulance is waiting."

"KIDNAPPING IS A CRIMINAL OFFENCE!" I shouted. I'd heard this on a police show recently. Kind of an obvious comment, if you thought about it, but I had to stall the removal of poor Mrs. Chewbley.

The stretcher bearers hesitated some more. The woken-up passengers began providing commentary.

"All those bandages. An odd way to travel, I must say. Rather like Cleopatra wrapping herself up in a carpet!"

"Is there even a hole for the poor thing to breathe through? Dreadful the way they treat old people nowadays."

"Wonder if that patient had the mussels. I was afraid to—I *knew* they looked a bit off."

Bundled in their housecoats, Talbot and Pantelli trotted up to me. Talbot murmured, "Okay, Di, what gives?"

I tried not to stare at Pantelli's housecoat, which was patterned with all kinds of trees, their Latin names underneath. "Edwina Chewbley is under those bandages!" I announced.

Jumping off the train, I marched up to the stretcher before Nurse Ballantyne could flare out a bony hand at me again. I grasped a bandage end. "Freedom is mere seconds away, Mrs. Chewbley."

With an authoritative nod at the porters, Freddy and the curious passengers now clogging the train doors, I peeled the head bandage off, round and round...

And round...

A face emerged, but not Mrs. Chewbley's.

The salt-and-pepper-haired woman's.

Freddy escorted Madge and me into the head conductor's office. "Way to pull a publicity stunt," the young conductor winked at me.

Then, having got his first good look at Madge, Freddy goggled while slo-o-owly closing the door. My sister, who'd changed into a pearl gray blouse and matching slacks, looked fresh and lovely, even at one in the morning—but this was a girl who looked fresh and lovely after playing tennis for two hours. Unnatural, if you ask me.

"Ow!" Still goggling, Freddy had closed the door on his nose.

The head conductor switched his unhappy gaze to me. "Forty-two years with the Gold-and-Blue," he mourned. "Never an incident like this. Never a claim about a disappearing passenger. Never an attack on a patient."

"Dinah didn't attack the patient," Madge pointed out. "She *unwrapped* her."

Though very critical of me herself, Madge grew prickly when others tried to be. It's a sister thing.

"Nurse Ballantyne's patient injured herself while rummaging in the luggage car for her extra set of dentures," Head Conductor Wiggins explained. "One of our cleaning staff opened the door for her, and she barged in ahead, without waiting for help. Said something about being 'dethperate.'

"She seems to have knocked over a stack of cartons, including a," Mr. Wiggins frowned at his notes, "box labeled Softie Toilet Paper. Odd. In any event, the falling boxes struck her on the head, jaw and ears, and she passed out. Nurse Ballantyne and I thought it best that she be moved to the nearest hospital."

"Very sensible and unmysterious," agreed Madge, with a stern sideways glance at me. "There will be no further trouble from my sister. *Will* there, Dinah?"

"Y'know, it's just so hard to commit," I began, and then I noticed the fierceness of Madge's glance. Blue as in glacial blue. "Er, no, there won't."

Chapter Fifteen
Charles? Chuck that Idea

Talbot, Pantelli and I poised our forks over the eggs Benedict. "Charge!" I ordered, and we all plunged our forks into the eggs at the same time. Yolks overran the plates like tsunamis. It was glorious, the true advantage of ordering eggs Benedict.

Madge was having her breakfast of grapefruit and melon wedges in our compartment. The baleful looks from other passengers gave her a headache, she'd said.

After stuffing a yolk-soaked English muffin in my mouth, I punched into Madge's cell phone—which I'd *borrowed*—the number from the envelope.

"This is Calvin Blimburg," a tinny voice said.

"Mflgmltch," I said.

"Sorry I'm not here right now. Got something to get rid of, huh? Without anyone knowing, I bet. Well, no probs. I'll deal with it, and we'll both stay mum."

"*Mflgmltch*," I repeated. The guy was a fence!

"Leave your name, or a phony name if you prefer, and I'll get back to you." Beep!

I gulped down the muffin. "I don't have a phony name," I said wrathfully. "And I don't approve of the business you're in. However, my dad wrote your number down, and I need to talk to you. My name's Dinah Galloway."

I added our number to the message and snapped the phone shut. Talbot was regarding me dubiously. "Do you really think you should give your personal contact info to a stranger, Di?"

I was too glum to worry about it. Had Dad handed over the king to Calvin Blimburg? Was that why it was missing from the envelope?

And why oh why had Dad contacted a fence in the first place? Whatever his other failings, I'd been sure Dad was honest.

In Winnipeg, everybody lined up for the tour bus that would first take us to Assiniboine Park and then to the famous Forks Market. At the prospect of shopping, Madge's mood improved, and she was chatting with another woman about the jewelry, pottery and other knickknacks from different cultures available at the market.

Pantelli glanced up from the *Plant Life of Assiniboine Park* brochure he was studying. "Dinah, how come you're being so quiet?"

I couldn't reply. I was too miserable at the thought of Dad getting involved with a fence.

Talbot rapped me gently on the head. "You in there, Di? I want to check on your walkie-talkie." Taking it from my hand, he pressed a duct-taped *On* switch. "Testing," he said into first my walkie-talkie, then his. "Testing..."

"We could always use them as doorstops," I said absently. I was looking at Pantelli's *Plant Life* brochure. One of the photos had distracted me, for the moment, from the thought of Dad and Calvin Blimburg.

I murmured to Pantelli and Talbot, "I've just had a blazingly brilliant idea about how to smoke out the Whisperer."

Talbot and I lowered our strings, each with a chunk of cheese tied at the end, into the green Assiniboine River. Madge, leaning against an elm, shook her head at us over her sketchbook.

"For all you know, prairie fish might *love* aged cheddar," I said defensively. Sitting cross-legged at the edge of the grassy bank, Talbot and I squinted into the green depths. Minnows were nipping at the cheese. Well, you had to start small.

The cheese was left over from the picnic Beanstalk had handed us when we boarded the Winnipeg tour bus. Though when Madge stepped in front of him, Beanstalk first clutched the basket to his heart. "Is it—can it be true you're engaged?" he demanded, with a catch in his voice.

I'd grabbed the basket from Beanstalk. "You're crushing our lunches."

"Not that there's anything wrong with being *un*engaged," I remarked now, as more minnows circled the cheese chunks. "In fact," I said loudly over my shoulder, "more and more people are choosing the solitary life."

"Yeah?" Talbot glanced at me sideways. "Is that what you're planning for yourself, Dinah?"

"I was thinking more of Madge," I said, raising my voice even more as my sister appeared to be dozing. "After all, true artists devote themselves to their work. ARTISTS LIKE MADGE," I bellowed.

Talbot grinned at me. "That's a relief. I mean," and he reached over to pull my string, which had drifted to the bank, back into the water, "think how solitary the solitary life would be."

From behind Madge in the bushes, *crackle*. That got her attention. Her blue eyes popped wide open. "Bears," she exclaimed fearfully and leapt up.

"You're so urban, Madge," I said, in withering tones. "That's no bear, it's Super Dendrologist."

Pantelli emerged from the bushes. He wore long gardening gloves, a full rain suit and a magnifying glass on a string around his neck. "I found just the specimens I wanted," he announced, holding up a Baggie filled with leaves.

Madge stared at him for a moment in disbelief. "Pantelli, it's a hot day. How can you stand to wear all that stuff? And aren't those your mother's gardening gloves?"

"They were," Pantelli informed her. Striding over to a trash bin, he peeled the gloves off, dropping them in without touching their outsides with his fingers. "When Mom opens her gardening shed, reaches inside for these and discovers them gone, she will just have to understand. People have to expect to make sacrifices in the name of science."

"I'm going for a walk," Madge said rather faintly.

We watched her stroll under some elms to the Winnie-the-Bear statue, sculpted in honor of the Winnipeg bear donated to the London Zoo in 1914. A.A. Milne named Winnie-the-Pooh after him.

Meanwhile, Pantelli stripped off his slicker so that he was just a regular kid in T-shirt and shorts again, not Super Dendrologist. He stuffed the rain jacket and pants into the bin.

"Good thing my sister didn't see that," I commented. "She would definitely have lectured you on wasting perfectly good clothes. And have asked inconvenient questions."

Good thing, as well, that Madge was so urban, I reflected. Otherwise she might've inspected the leaves in the plastic bag and recognized them as poison ivy.

Phase one of my blazingly brilliant idea, or BBI, was now complete.

We stood in front of *The Path of Time*, a sculpture by Marcel Gosselin at the entrance to the Forks Market. The sun-shaped sculpture let light in through carved-out symbols.

Light filtered through different symbols depending on where the sun sat, high in summer, low in winter.

"Just think, people have been gathering at the forks of the Red and Assiniboine rivers for six thousand years," Madge mused. She already had her sketchbook out.

"But only one of them is the Whisperer," I muttered to Talbot and Pantelli.

I'd jammed the walkie-talkie into a back pocket of my cutoffs. Signs warned about pickpockets, but I wasn't worried about losing the walkie-talkie. Like, who'd want it? "This is what I'm anxious to hold on to," I practically shouted and held up my rainbow purse.

"So *loud*, Dinah," Madge tsked, unaware that drawing attention to my purse was all part of my BBI. She flipped her sketchbook shut and traced the arc of the inner limestone sculpture with her finger. "Birth, life and death. From the earth, and back to the earth."

"Uh, Madge, if you don't mind, we're hoping not to spend the birth-life-death span *here*..."

Madge sighed. "The way it's turning out, much of my own lifespan consists of listening to Mother and Mrs. Audia plan my wedding."

I peered unhappily at Madge. "That may come to an end pretty soon."

It was now time for phase two of my BBI.

"Of course I'll be fine," I assured Madge. "I'll be with Talbot and Pantelli. I know you would much rather prowl blissfully through the two levels of market stalls and shops on your own."

Besides, I thought, we have to get rid of you to make my idea work.

"We-ell…" Madge hesitated. She gave an odd glance at Pantelli, still brandishing his Baggie of leaves. Then her glance fell on Talbot, and she smiled. Grown-ups always trusted Talbot. "All right. We'll meet back here in an hour." Noticing a stall glistening with First Nations silver jewelry, she broke into an Olympic sprint.

After a brief BBI strategy meeting, Talbot, Pantelli and I headed past limestone etchings of Manitoba's past: the lined, weary faces of the immigrants, and the logo of the North West fur-trade company, with a spreading oak tree and the word *PERSEVERANCE* overhead.

Perseverance. I studied the immigrants' faces and vowed, *I'll* persevere and find you, Mrs. Chewbley.

"Almost more of a plane tree look," Pantelli murmured, inspecting the etched tree through his magnifying glass. We yanked him away.

I walked ahead of the boys. Swinging my rainbow purse, I passed stalls with wooden animal sculptures, brightly beaded necklaces and bracelets, and swirled glasswork vases that flashed red, yellow, blue in the sun pouring through the skylights.

Then, all at once, it was the colors of stamps that were flashing: ribbons of them in shrink-wrap, fluttering as visitors brushed by. "How much would an elk stamp be worth?" I blurted to the red-faced man behind the counter.

With angry glances up at the skylight, the stamp dealer was busy smearing sun block over his cheeks. He squished some more out of a bottle, *ble-e-ah-ttt,* and rubbed it into his forehead. "I've complained and complained about this location. I shouldn't be under the sun—not me or my stamps! Bad for both of us. I burn, they fade!" The stamp dealer slammed the bottle on the counter.

He turned to me. "So ya got an elk," he grunted. "The elk stamp came out several years ago. A big bright one. Fine stamp. It'd be worth..." He scratched his chin.

"Eighty thousand dollars?"

The stamp dealer's features, shiny with cream, scrunched into a scowl. "Are you funnin' with me, kid? A *dollar* eighty I'd give you, max."

"I thought so," I said. "But what about a stamp with a king on it? Say, King Charles the First?"

The dealer's lotioned features gathered into a shiny scowl. "Now I *know* you're funnin' with me, kid. That King Charles, the guy who lost his head, came way before stamps were invented.

"See, in Britain, it used to be that if you sent a letter, the person receiving the letter had to pay for it. Well, you can guess what happened. A lot of people refused, and the poor mail carrier was stuck with them. Some people even arranged with their buddies to put secret messages in the *address* of the letter. That way, the recipient could glance at the address on the outside, read the secret message and hand the letter back without ever having to pay."

Happy to be chatting about his favorite topic, the stamp dealer forgot to be angry about the direct sunlight beating on him. "In 1837, Rowland Hill suggested the *senders* start paying. Three years later, the first stamp appeared. It was called the 'penny black' because its portrait of Queen Victoria was printed in black. Shell out one penny, and your letter would go anywhere in the British Isles! Finally, the British had a system that worked. *The penny dropped*, you might say." The stamp dealer's shoulders shook with laughter at his joke.

"Hmm," I said, disappointed. "I was hoping Charles might be on a valuable stamp."

The stamp dealer wiped his eyes with a tissue. "Valuable? I'll tell you what's valuable: the 1855 Swedish three-skilling stamp. Now *that's* worth a pretty penny. 'Penny'!" Reminded of his joke, the dealer started laughing again, till I scowled at him.

He sighed. "The stamp was supposed to be printed in green, but due to a mistake it came out yellow. That mistake made the 1855 three-skilling very rare. In 1996, somebody bought one for 2.3 million dollars. A stamp with a blooper is guaranteed to be valuable because just a few are issued before printing is halted."

The stamp dealer fished a crumpled business card out of his wallet and handed it to me. "Now, if you ever come up with a blooper skilling stamp, lemme know."

I looked around. Talbot and Pantelli were catching up to me. They made circular forefinger movements beside their heads: *Are you crazy?* The plan was for me to stay in front of them.

I pushed ahead and immediately got entangled in long scarves of polka dots, glittery silver, fiery sequins, all suspended from hangers.

"Just a minute," the scarf-stall owner objected. "What do you think you're doing, young lady? Those are my wares, *not* training equipment for you to practice rhythmic gymnastics on."

"I don't mean to," I protested, unwinding myself from a white scarf with a smiling blue puffin on it. "I'm trying to get out..."

But the more I tried, the more I became wrapped up in scarves. *Someone was spinning the scarves around me.* Tighter and tighter they grew. I was eyeball to eyeball with the smiling puffin.

"I'll take that purse," whispered a voice on the other side of the puffin. The voice from the observation dome. The Whisperer!

And my purse was plucked from my hand. Was the Whisperer Nurse Ballantyne, as I suspected? I couldn't see, couldn't even reach after it. Scarves bound my arms to my sides, mummy style.

Talbot chased after the thief. Pantelli stayed to unwrap the scarves and drop them carelessly on the ground as the stall owner fumed.

"Did you see who it was?" I demanded when my head was free of the puffin scarf.

"Somebody in a trench coat, hat and gloves," Pantelli said unhelpfully. He paused to admire a scarf with trees on it. "Ah yes, our old friend, the horse chestnut. We have these at home, in Vancouver," he explained to the stall owner, who glared back. "The horse chestnut has medicinal properties if used correctly. If not, well..." Pantelli waggled his eyebrows ominously.

The stall owner exploded, "Your friend's purse has been stolen, my scarves are getting dumped on the ground *and you're talking about trees*?!"

Pantelli glanced at her curiously. "What else would you like to talk about?"

Talbot sprinted up to us, hardly out of breath at all, I noticed irritably. Talbot was one of those types who sprinted round the school track even when not ordered to by a gym teacher. Like, for *fun*.

Jack did that kind of thing too—but Jack was an even more disagreeable subject to me these days than athletics, so I shoved him out of my mind.

"Your whispering thief got away," Talbot apologized. "He or she was pretty cunning about it too—hid behind a book rack. Then stuck a fist out and punched me."

Talbot was squinting at us out of one eye. The skin around it was dandelion yellow; soon it would be a bright purple.

"You're going to have a fine shiner," I said, crooking

my arm through his. "We better find you some ice. Look, there's a sno-cone vendor over there. You can snack while cooling your shiner down."

Pantelli chimed in, "My aunt gave me a bag of frozen peas for *my* shiner last month." He added, for the stall owner's benefit, "Friends of Di tend to accumulate injuries."

The stall owner was busy gathering her scarves up off the ground. She flapped several of them at us. "You ought to be telling the police about the stolen purse."

"Oh, we'll know who the thief is soon enough," I called over my shoulder as Pantelli and I led Talbot to the sno-cone vendor. "The stolen purse is filled with poison ivy."

"At least we know now that, whatever the valuable King Charles item is, it can't possibly be a stamp," I said on the bus back from the Forks. "Charles the First was pre-stamp."

Pantelli nodded. Talbot probably would have too, except that he was leaning his head back against his seat, with a bag of ice jammed over his shiner.

Pantelli informed us smugly, "You may be interested to know the species of oak that Charles the Second was hiding in. I've been Googling, and it was an oak *apple* tree at Boscobel House. A descendant of the oak apple lives at Boscobel to this day. That's the benefit," Pantelli added, nodding wisely, "of preserving acorns."

"Strange," Talbot uttered in a muffled voice from under his ice pack. "My headache's actually getting *worse*."

Madge was a few seats ahead, comparing purchases with a couple of other women. I punched our home number into her cell.

Mother came on the line and cooed how much she missed me, reminded me to behave, and blathered other Motherly nonsense. "Oh, and I visited Ardle today. I got a word or two out of him about this king you asked about."

"Yeah?"

"Yes, not yeah, Dinah. Anyhow, Ardle mumbled that this king—"

"Yeah? I mean, yes?"

"—is a stamp."

Chapter Sixteen

Madge Burns About LaFlamme

Madge slid her engagement ring up and down her finger. "I can't understand it," she fretted. "The only e-mail I've received from Jack today is a group one saying how shallow and boring he is."

Madge and I were in our compartment. The Gold-and-Blue was swiftly skimming from Manitoba into northern Ontario. The scenery had roused itself from flat prairie. Trees now crowded the sides of the tracks.

I said, "Sometimes young men have changes of personality, Madge. It could be that Jack is, well, shifting."

"You make him sound like a tectonic plate." Madge pulled off the ring and studied it as if trying to read her future in the tiny diamond's lights and shadows. "Is there something you're not telling me, Dinah?"

"Ummm..."

"There is." Madge rounded on me, her blue eyes bright with anger and tears. "Out with it, Dinah Mary Galloway. *What is it that I don't know about Jack?*"

"Ummm..." Best to break it to Madge tactfully.

Except that I've never quite grasped the tact concept.

"Jack is two-timing you."

"What were those blood-curdling screams?" Talbot inquired as I stepped out of the compartment and met him and Pantelli.

"Madge, finding out about Jack and Veronica LaFlamme." I shook my head. "Jack, of all people! I still can't believe it."

However, there was no time to ponder Jack's fall—make that kamikaze descent—from our good graces. Talbot, Pantelli and I had poison ivy to investigate.

"There's nothing like a gross rash to flush out a suspect," Pantelli remarked in satisfaction as we bustled along the passageways to the infirmary. The Whisperer just had to be stretched out on one of Nurse Ballantyne's cots.

We had a ready-made excuse for knocking on the infirmary door: Pantelli and his motion sickness. As a matter of fact, the Gold-and-Blue skimmed along so smoothly he hadn't barfed since the wee episode in the observation car—but there was no need to let Nurse Ballantyne know this.

The infirmary was fully lighted. Two cots with their starched, sterilized linens gleamed brightly. We peered round. No Nurse Ballantyne.

And yet I felt someone's presence.

"We'll grow roots if we keep standing here," I whispered and began tiptoeing toward the desk. I figured Nurse Ballantyne had to keep a record book of patients.

Talbot grabbed my elbow. He pointed over the cots to what I'd assumed was a wall. At closer glance, I saw it was a floor-to-ceiling white plastic curtain drawn fully across the room. Against the curtain, the silhouette of a large bony hand lifted, grabbed a bottle and then flopped down again. A moan echoed through the infirmary. Pantelli turned as white as the curtain. "So...has it actually been *proven* that the dead don't walk?"

"Shhh!" I hissed.

The three of us crept toward the curtain. I was the nearest to the curtain's edge. I touched it with a baby finger and crooked it ever so gently aside.

In a green hospital gown, Nurse Ballantyne lay on a cot, eyes shut and horselike face covered with huge, angry red splotches. A bottle of calamine lotion was clutched in an equally splotchy hand.

Talbot, Pantelli and I dropped our jaws in unison. Who says junior sleuthing doesn't provide you with good exercise?

This confirmed my suspicions. Nurse Ballantyne *was* the Whisperer.

We ducked into a nearby linen supply room to discuss this latest development. Pantelli grabbed a facecloth and mopped his forehead. "Dendrology doesn't take it out of you the way sleuthing does," he moaned.

Talbot said, "The train gets into Toronto tomorrow afternoon. What if we haven't found Mrs. Chewbley by then? Do they smuggle her off, never to be seen again? Reminds me of the case of the Princes in the Tower in 1483. The two princes vanished, probably murdered."

Normally I enjoyed these ghoulish historical anecdotes of Talbot's, but I shuddered on Mrs. Chewbley's behalf. After Head Conductor Wiggins's search had turned up no Mrs. Chewbley, he and his staff concluded she'd definitely disembarked at Jasper. *I* knew they were wrong.

"We have to find her," I declared.

Talbot nodded. "We know that only one person, a patient, has left the train. Therefore, Mrs. Chewbley must still be on the Gold-and-Blue, but not anywhere the crew has looked. Okay. Where would you stash a woman you didn't want anyone else to find?"

"The men's washroom?" Pantelli suggested.

I hoisted myself on a huge hamper and began swinging my legs so that *thunk*! *thunk*! my heels hit the sides. Noise always helps me think. "The luggage car," I speculated. "At the start of the trip, that's where you have the conductor store anything you won't need. Like your leaf specimens, Pantelli. You know they'll be safe *because the luggage car is kept locked*."

Talbot grinned at me. "Another blazingly brilliant deduction from our favorite girl sleuth. As a Gold-and-Blue employee, Nurse Ballantyne would most likely have access to the luggage-car key."

I was really smashing the sides of the hamper now. "I bet that poor dentures woman wasn't accidentally knocked on the head. I bet someone slammed a box on her because, while prowling around for her spare dentures, she saw something she shouldn't have."

"That does it, Pantelli," Talbot said. "You and I are going to approach Freddy and ask in our politest possible manner if we can check on how your leaves are doing."

"What about me?" I demanded. "It may surprise you, Talbot St. John, but I, too, am able to muster a polite manner now and then."

"Ha!" Pantelli scoffed. "If so, it'd be harder to find than Mrs. Chewbley."

"Yeah? This from the guy who thought *24* would be improved if the title referred to tree rings instead of hours!"

"Puh-leeze, you two," Talbot begged. "Dinah, you're a target. I think we should escort you safely back to your compartment, where you double-bolt the door."

I opened my mouth to object, specifically to the word "safely," which I always find tedious.

Talbot cut me off. "Besides, Madge is upset about Jack and this LaCrème woman."

"La*Flamme*."

"Whatever. Anyhow, at this trying time for Madge,

you should be there in case she wakes up and needs you to comfort her."

"Crafty, very crafty," I informed Talbot. "Knowing that I have no sense of natural caution, you appeal to my sense of guilt."

"Which you have in spades," Talbot said comfortably. His dark eyes twinkled at me.

It was still early evening, as in pre-prowl time, so we took Ryan to the games car for a game of ping-pong. He was getting pretty good. He sailed the ball right between Talbot and Pantelli and he grinned at my wild cheers—but still didn't say anything.

After, we all flopped down at a booth. "Nurse Ballantyne isn't the only one who can *wompf!* people," I informed Ryan. "You *wompf!* ping-pong balls."

Ryan mouthed the word *wompf!* He liked it.

Freddy wheeled up a cart with water bottles; we each grabbed one. I decided to pour everyone's water into glasses. Of course I managed to slosh water on the table. Why couldn't I pour in a queenly manner, like my sister?

A queen. A *king*, I thought. Always back to that.

"So tell us, oh wise historian," I said to Talbot. "Charles the First was too early to appear on a stamp. What other king got beheaded?"

Talbot took a long glug of water before replying. "The difficulty is, all this hacking off of monarchs' heads occurred before stamps were invented. There was Mary, Queen of

Scots, in 1587, Charles the First in 1649, France's Louis the Sixteenth and Marie Antoinette in 1793..."

Shrugging, he took another long slurp and drained his glass. "Unless you count Russia's Czar Nicholas and Czarina Alexandra and their whole family in 1918, but they were shot, not beheaded."

"Please," I begged, holding up my hands. Pantelli and I savored this type of history lesson, but I could see Ryan's dark eyes growing rounder and rounder. I didn't want him to have nightmares. "I can see I lost my head, as it were, in asking you."

"Bad pun alert," Pantelli chanted.

The bad pun circled back, Frisbee-like, to my mind. Which was where a light suddenly flashed on. How stupid I'd been!

"Talbot," I said, my voice rather shaky, "forget about kings who had their heads chopped off. Was there ever a king who lost his head as in," I struggled to say it right, "acting foolishly or impulsively?"

Talbot paused in aiming his empty bottle at a recycle bin. "Oh, sure," he said, surprised, as if I'd asked him something so easy it was hardly worth mentioning. "Edward the Eighth. Handsome guy. Smooth-talking, witty, fashion plate-ish...Edward fell like a ton of bricks for some American dame nobody approved of. In 1936 he gave up his crown to marry her."

Edward the Eighth! Why hadn't I asked the right question before? I clutched my head, marveling at the dim-wittedness it contained. "How silly!"

Talbot pulled away my glass, which I'd almost

elbow-swiped off the table. "I dunno if Edward was *silly*," he said. "If you like someone, you tend to put up with a lot."

I sensed that, in a vague way, he was referring to putting up with *me*, and I felt oddly pleased. I managed a weak, rueful grin.

Chapter Seventeen

Another Passenger Disappears

I climbed into bed fully clothed in case I had to rush out to help Talbot and Pantelli. If only they could find poor old Mrs. Chewbley! From under my pillow I withdrew the mega-canister of Smarties that I'd bought from the snack shop. I'd planned to gobble down the contents as a pre-breakfast treat while waiting for Madge to beautify herself—a long and, in my view, completely unnecessary process. But, out of sheer nervousness, I started eating the Smarties now.

Poor Mrs. Chewbley! What if *she* wasn't getting enough to eat? I tucked back more and more Smarties. I was picturing Mrs. Chewbley: on my piano bench, rewarding me with orange creams even when I'd bashed the keys out of all proportion to the Edna May Oliver tune; crunching over our horse chestnuts in search of her glasses; beaming patiently at Pantelli as he blathered on about his tree "findings."

Madge turned over in bed, blinked at the lamplight and woke up. "Oh, hi. I'm glad—though slightly stunned—that you junior sleuths are actually keeping to a curfew. No late-night prowling or anything like that."

"Ummm..."

"You may be interested to know that I finally got through to Jack's cell." Madge sat up, managed a wan smile and burst into tears.

This didn't sound promising. I waited glumly for her to continue.

"He said—he said he wanted me to be open-minded. Then," Madge shook her head, almost unable to go on, "*he hung up!*"

At this point her tears turned into agonized howls. I squeezed her hand, feeling, A, terrible for her, B, even more furious at Jack than before, and, C, uneasy about the sleep prospects for the people in the neighboring compartments.

I switched the light off so Madge could howl herself to sleep and waited outside in the passageway for Pantelli and Talbot to return.

In the meantime, unfolding the stamp dealer's card, I punched in his number on Madge's cell.

"Yeah?" he barked into the phone.

"Um, hi. This is Dinah Galloway. I'm the one with the elk stamp."

Gusty sigh. "I told you, kid. A dollar eighty for it, and that's final."

"I don't want to sell the elk," I said hastily. "I'm phoning to ask you if there's a King Edward the Eighth stamp worth eighty thousand dollars."

Loud snort in my ear. "The King Edward the Eighth blooper? Maybe it was worth eighty grand a few years ago. We're talking out-in-orbit prices now, kid. The King Eddie ain't as big and colorful as a lot of the ones they make now, but it's worth millions."

Practically staggering under all this information, I squeaked, "So there *was* a King Edward blooper stamp!"

"Sure. The stamp was issued showing Edward at his coronation. Y'know, the official crowning of a king or queen."

"What's the blooper in that?"

"You being cute with me, kid? The blooper was that *the coronation never happened*. Eddie quit the throne to marry his girlfriend in December 1936."

"Holy Toledo."

"There's no Holy Toledo about it. What'd I tell you at the market? Blooper stamps are the most valuable because so few of 'em get printed.

"Now leave me alone. I gotta watch me some baseball."

The door to our car banged open. I was still standing outside the door of Madge's and my compartment, wondering what to do next. Pantelli trudged up to me with a horse chestnut branch. "Found this in the luggage car. It appears I'm not the only dendrologist aboard the Gold-and-Blue."

He paused at the sound of the howling. "Wow, you can really hear the coyotes at night."

"That's Madge. Let's just say she's not adapting well to the single life." I pushed away the branch, with its lone, spiky-shelled horse chestnut dangling like a Christmas tree ornament. "So what happened in the luggage car?"

"I replaced the ice packs in my specimen case," Pantelli reported happily. He wagged the branch some more. "Whoever the other dendrologist is, he's not being as careful as I am. Proves he doesn't read *Young Dendrologist* magazine."

With waning patience, I demanded, "What did *Talbot* find in the luggage car?"

Pantelli regarded me owlishly. "I dunno. Didn't he tell you?"

I was close to erupting in Madge-like howls myself. "I haven't seen Talbot."

"Huh. I thought he'd headed back here. I was busy arranging my Baggies of *Aesculus hippocastanum* leaves. When I finished, I looked around and no Talbot."

Pantelli put down the horse chestnut branch he'd been studying. Our eyes widened at each other. We shoved open the door to Talbot's and Pantelli's compartment.

Empty.

For the second time aboard the Gold-and-Blue, a passenger had disappeared.

Chapter Eighteen

The Luggage Car, a.k.a. the Black Hole

"No," pleaded Head Conductor Wiggins. In his gold-trimmed blue dressing gown, with a head conductor's badge sewn on the breast pocket, he leaned against the doorframe. "Not another missing-person report. You wouldn't do that to me, Miss Galloway. You *wouldn't*."

Freddy, who'd escorted Pantelli and me to the head conductor's compartment, beamed. "I gotta hand it to you, Miss Galloway. You sure crank out the PR stunts."

"Talbot has disappeared," I said urgently. "We have to search the train."

Head Conductor Wiggins covered his face with his hands. Moans limped out from behind his fingers. "This can't be happening. Did you check the games room? The library? The observation dome?"

"Well, no," I admitted. "But why would Talbot go any

of those places in the middle of an investigation? I can't see him sitting down to play chess by himself," I added witheringly.

"If so, he's winning very handily," Pantelli pointed out, wagging his horse chestnut branch.

Head Conductor Wiggins parted his fingers to peer out at us through bloodshot eyes. "Young Mr. St. John is playing a prank on you, Miss Galloway. It's what boys do when they like a girl. I remember such things from my own youth.

"My youth," the head conductor repeated on a sob. "You'd never believe, to look at me now—weak, defeated—that I was once young, would you?"

"No," Pantelli agreed cheerfully. He was using the dangling horse chestnut and branch as a paddleball toy; now, after a particularly vigorous bounce against the branch, the gourd-encased chestnut flew loose. It wheeled toward Head Conductor Wiggins—and one of its spikes gouged his earlobe.

"AAAGGGHHH!"

"Sir, maybe you'd prefer we come back later," Freddy suggested.

"Yeah, like 2012," the head conductor moaned, prying the spike from his flesh.

"I just don't believe Talbot would abandon you in the luggage car," I told Pantelli. "It's not like him. He's too conscientious and honorable."

We were in the dining car, at the table where I'd last

seen Mrs. Chewbley. Freddy showed up with mugs of black coffee.

We both grimaced at the taste of the coffee. It was more than strong. It was Herculean. Yech. But we wanted to make ourselves stay awake to search for Talbot.

"I sure wish I'd paid more attention," Pantelli lamented. "I was concentrating on the stria of my poplar leaves."

"Is that like, stria-k, you're out?" inquired Freddy.

"Stria are the lines on leaves," Pantelli told him. "Fascinating. Why, I once spent five and a half hours examining the stria of an—"

"Never mind," I said wearily. "And it's not your fault you got distracted. It's just the way you tree types are."

"Dendrologists," Pantelli corrected.

Ignoring him, I begged Freddy, "Will you puh-leeze let us in the luggage car one more time? I think Talbot found something there. If I can find out what it is, maybe I'll know why he and Mrs. Chewbley have both disappeared."

"When you're done, come find me and I'll lock up," Freddy instructed. "Tootles!" He sauntered off.

Just inside the luggage car door, Pantelli and I hesitated. We didn't actually have a plan—a weakness that seems to feature in much of my sleuthing.

The gold-tiled passageway continued down the luggage car, only with stacks of suitcases, huge trunks standing on end, and cartons of all sizes instead of compartments. There was a stuffy stillness to the luggage car that should have convinced me no one else was there, but didn't. Pantelli whispered hoarsely, "Do you get the feeling we're not alone?"

"I'm hoping it's just spiders I sense here," I whispered back. Gulping, I nudged him. "C'mon, as long as we use the buddy system, we'll be okay."

We moved past some boxes labeled *PETRIE'S PORCELAIN DOLLS*. The boxes weren't large enough to hold a person—at least, not a whole one. I shuddered. That was it. After this, I was rationing my reading of Deathstalkers comics.

Pantelli elbowed me. "Look at this carton!"

It was a giant ebony box that stretched from floor to ceiling. On the side, in ghoulish, dripping-candle-wax-like letters, it said: *HANS & ROMAN, THE WORLD-FAMOUS MAGICIANS, PRESENT THEIR SPECIAL DISAPPEARING COFFIN*!

I stared. I knew Hans and Roman. They'd performed their mega-magic show on the same Alaska cruise ship I'd sung on this past May. Without intending to, I'd sort of upstaged them—but they'd been good sports about it, since I'd got extremely cold, wet and uncomfortable in the process. We'd even talked about working together sometime.

Suddenly, any fond memories I was indulging in were interrupted by a deafening "WOO-HOO!"

Yelping in shock, Pantelli and I fell backward against Hans and Roman's magic coffin.

"WOO-HOO!"

About to let out a second scream, I looked up—and saw a giant wooden cuckoo poised over me. Bright blue, with gleaming red eyes, it was jutting out on a pole from a doghouse-sized clock wedged atop a steamer trunk. It was doing the *Woo-Hoo* song as opposed to an old-fashioned cuckoo sound.

"WOO-HOO, WOO-HOO-HOO!"

Crackle.

Huh? Wait, that crackle wasn't part of the *Woo-Hoo* tune. It was...I wrenched the walkie-talkie out of my back pocket. *Crackle.* Gad, the thing actually worked.

I flipped the light switch that served as the *On* button. "Talbot?"

"WOO-HOO!" the cuckoo shrieked above me.

"Dinah, stay away from the luggage car..."

"It's a bit late for that," I informed Talbot. "Where are you? I've been so worried, my stomach's in sailor's knots. You're not the type to wander off, not like me. I'm supposed to be able to *count* on you."

His next words were barely intelligible. "...got me. I'm in with the..." *crackle* "...dolls."

My gaze veered to the boxes labeled *PETRIE'S PORCELAIN DOLLS*. Poor Talbot must be squished up like a pretzel if he were in one of those. I ran toward them and began yanking randomly at the boxes. "*Who* got you, Talbot?"

A particularly ear-splitting *crackle*, and the walkie-talkie lapsed into silence.

A weirdly intense silence. After a moment, I realized why. The loudmouth cuckoo had finally shut up and retreated behind his bright red wooden door.

It was odd that Pantelli wasn't clambering up to check what wood the door was made of.

I looked around. Odder still that Pantelli wasn't anywhere near me.

I gulped. "Pantelli? Uh, remember what we agreed about the buddy system?"

The ceiling lamps, flat and pale as blank pages, gleamed up and down the gold-tiled motionless passageway. Nobody there.

I gulped again. First Mrs. Chewbley, then Talbot, then Pantelli. All vanished. Maybe this wasn't the Gold-and-Blue at all. Maybe it was the Black Hole.

I would've started biting my nails, except that I'd chomped them down to the quick that morning as part of my regular manicure routine. Nope, I'd have to go for Option B, always the last resort of a junior sleuth: taking the problem to a grown-up. Head Conductor Wiggins would be so-o-o pleased to hear that a third passenger had disappeared.

I started back to the luggage car entrance.

And stopped.

Whistling pierced the air. Beautifully pitched whistling, flute-like.

Hey, I knew that tune—

Black socks, they never get dirty,

The longer you wear them
The blacker they get.

It was coming from the far end of the luggage car.

Someday I think I will wash them,
But something keeps telling me...

Something was telling me to escape the luggage car now. To do the sensible thing and find a grown-up. A whole pack of grown-ups, preferably.

Don't do it yet.

But—what else is new?—my curiosity was too much for me. Who was whistling my song, the one I'd been singing when I first met Ardle McBean, seven years ago? My feet began moving to the far end of the luggage car, drawn by that Pied Piper-style whistling.

Not yet, not yet.

Past rows of jammed-in steamer trunks, the whistling grew stronger, swept around me like the eddy of a sweet, irresistible current, filled my eardrums...

I was beside a green-with-gold-trim trunk. Standing on its side, the trunk was so long it practically qualified as a train car itself. I placed a palm against the shiny surface.

Black socks...

The whistling reverberated into my hand and right through me.

I slid my hand over to a gold latch. My fingers closed on it. Nothing to be afraid of. After all, I thought, what kind of villain would *whistle*? I pulled on the latch, and it swung open like a door.

The trunk didn't have a back to it. A large rectangle had been cut out. I could see right through to the other side.

Where Mrs. Chewbley sat, drinking tea at a table.

Chapter Nineteen

The Mad Hatter Had Nothing on this Tea Party

I did the only thing I ever do when intensely surprised. I wisecracked.

"Does the baggage handlers' union know about this?"

Mrs. Chewbley held out her arms. "I knew you'd find me! That's why I was happily whistling that tune you're always singing. I was thinking of you and not worrying at all. You're such a clever girl."

I edged round the table and let myself be enfolded in a soft lavender-scented hug. "Mrs. Chewbley, let's get out of here! Both Talbot and Pantelli are missing, but now that I've found you, I can prove—"

Ping! Ping! Hairpins cascaded, some landing on a large wicker picnic basket, some sliding down the side of a plump gold and blue teapot and onto fainting-women romance novels scattered on the floor. The piano teacher was shaking her head slowly, sadly. "You can't leave, Dinah. The trunk flapped shut behind you—and it only opens from the outside."

I spun, knocking against the table so that the teapot lid danced and clattered. Mrs. Chewbley was right. The trunk door was stuck fast, no matter how hard I pushed it.

"Bowl Cut's just cleverer than we are," Mrs. Chewbley shrugged. She produced another cup from a nearby box and poured tea out for me. "Peppermint tea. You'll love it. So good with chocolate creams!"

I saw that yet another box was stacked with dirty cups and dishes. For a fleeting second I was reminded of the Mad Hatter's tea party. Then I reminded myself that Mrs. Chewbley was a prisoner; the setting was hardly her own choice.

Mrs. Chewbley smiled sadly. "While you were napping in the dining car, Bowl Cut crept up behind me, covered my face with a chloroform-doused cloth," she leaned forward and lowered her voice ominously, "and dragged me off."

I'd read up on chloroform for a report to last month's Neighborhood Block Watch meeting. (Funny—the meetings were getting smaller each month. Good thing *I* was such a steadfast attendee.) I adjusted my glasses thoughtfully. "Chloroform stinks. I'm surprised the smell didn't wake me up."

Mrs. Chewbley reached inside the basket for a deviled egg sandwich. "Maybe you were too tired to wake up." She took a large chomp.

"But," I objected—Mother and Madge often complained that "but" was my favorite word—"wouldn't someone have seen Bowl Cut dragging you off? Beanstalk was in the dining car. Maybe he's part of this too." I sighed. "Are there many people on the planet who *aren't*?"

"Or maybe Bowl Cut bribed him." Mrs. Chewbley waved the remaining crescent of egg sandwich at me. "Bowl Cut is ruthless, Dinah."

I sank down on a carton labeled *GARDEN ORNAMENTS: SOLID STONE! LARGER THAN LIFE!* since there weren't any other chairs. "I haven't even spotted Bowl Cut on this train. Some junior sleuth I am."

"Oh, no," Mrs. Chewbley soothed. "You're a very good sleuth, Dinah—just over your head on this one. Here, let me find you some creamer for your tea." Whistling, she rummaged in the picnic basket.

I was in full self-pity mode by now. "Sherlock Holmes wouldn't have snoozed while a material witness was kidnapped," I mourned. "And, in the best Pantelli Audia tradition, I felt ready to heave when I woke up. Not very suave."

Woo-hoo, woo-hoo-hoo. Mrs. Chewbley was whistling the cuckoo's tune now. In her search for the creamers, she was withdrawing more sandwiches, fruit, chocolate creams...Bowl Cut certainly kept his prisoners well fed.

Much as I liked Mrs. Chewbley, found her a food soul mate and all that, I couldn't help thinking that Mr. Wellman would have been a way better match for Bowl Cut. Though in his late fifties, my agent worked out daily at a gym. Rather than allowing himself to be dragged off, the lean, agile Mr. W. would have landed a few good punches on Bowl Cut's smug, dinner-plate face.

Mr. Wellman would also have dealt much better with Head Conductor Wiggins than I had. Being loud and tactless, I tended to alienate authority figures. Smooth Mr. Wellman charmed them practically to purring.

If only Mr. Wellman hadn't got sick!

Still whistling *Woo-Hoo* in her beautiful pitch, Mrs. Chewbley pulled out a squashed nougat bar in her quest for creamer.

But, I thought regretfully, Mr. Wellman had caught the flu from that would-be client, the one he'd told me about on the phone. Not even a very promising client at that, he'd said. One who whistled.

I gaped at Mrs. Chewbley. *A whistler had visited my agent.* Had breathed all over his lunch, and he'd promptly got sick, preventing him from making the train trip.

Got sick. I'd heard this refrain before, from Mother, about Mrs. Grimsbottom.

Pantelli's regular piano teacher got sick, so Mrs. Chewbley, a new neighbor down the street, has taken over his lessons for the summer. She's very nice, not like that sour old Mrs. Grimsbottom. Mrs. Chewbley has offered to give you lessons too, Dinah. Apparently she has the patience of a saint.

I'd replied, *Oh, ha ha ha, Mother*. What I was

thinking now was, Oh, ho-ho-hold on. Mr. Wellman, Mrs. Grimsbottom. In both cases, they'd got sick—and Mrs. Chewbley had stepped forward, beaming, as a substitute.

Did Mrs. Chewbley have something to do with their getting sick? Rather than breathing on Mr. Wellman's lunch, she could've added something to it when he wasn't looking. Could've just pretended to be sick herself.

Nooo. Far-fetched, Dinah. Not likely.

Well, not very likely.

But suppose she *had* poisoned them. In that case, Mrs. Chewbley wasn't quite the sweet old lady she seemed.

In that case, she might be involved with the people trying to get hold of the stamp.

I thought rapidly. Mrs. Chewbley had moved into our neighborhood just before Ardle got out of jail. Did she know he'd head for our house? Was she tracking down the stamp by keeping watch on Ardle—and on us?

"What are you thinking, Dinah?" twinkled Mrs. Chewbley.

"Ummm. About what a nice piano teacher you've been to Pantelli and me."

Too nice, I thought all of a sudden. Would a proper piano teacher praise every single note Pantelli played, when, with no Mrs. Grimsbottom to bully him, he'd been slacking off for the past few weeks? Would a proper piano teacher fail to object when I bashed out my Edna May Oliver exercises so deafeningly?

R-r-rip! Tearing open the creamer packet, Mrs. Chewbley

sprinkled the contents into my teacup. "Poor child, you're pale! This tea will have you right as rain in no time."

I stared at my reflection in the tea. Then I wasn't seeing my reflection, but rather Mrs. Chewbley prowling about in our front yard under the horse chestnut trees. Looking for her glasses, she'd explained.

But maybe she'd really been looking for something else.

For horse chestnuts.

Horse chestnuts are way too bitter to eat, unlike sweet chestnuts, Pantelli had said. *Toxic and poisonous...The effect all depends on the dose...*

He'd also said, *Mrs. Chewbley's cool. Unlike Mrs. Grimsbottom, she doesn't mind when I rant on about trees.*

She didn't mind—because she was busy listening and learning.

I gulped. All at once I knew that under no circumstances should I drink this tea.

"Drink up, dear," Mrs. Chewbley said brightly. A little too brightly. Her tiny, currant-like eyes were brilliant, and her cheeks burned with two scarlet points.

The steam from the teacup roiled up to my face. I blinked at it—and my eyelids almost stayed shut. I was exhausted. I wanted, oh how I wanted, to oblige Mrs. Chewbley by knocking the tea back and sleeping for a hundred years. Naw, not a hundred. That'd be a mere catnap. Sleeping Beauty got ripped off. I wanted to sleep for the next millennium.

Mrs. Chewbley pushed the teacup closer to me. "Drink *up*, Dinah."

My groggy brain was hatching a plan. A lame plan, but a plan. It was so very lame it just might work.

"Mrs. Chewbley," I said, "there's a huge black spider right behind you."

The piano teacher gave me a broad, knowing smile. "A spider," she repeated. With a faint shrug, she turned.

I grasped the handles of the two teacups, hers and mine, and pushed the cups around. When she turned back, the tea in both cups was bouncing. Would she notice?

The piano teacher's smile, now revealing small, rather pointed teeth, was downright unpleasant. It must've always been, except that she'd covered it with cute twittering and lots and *lots* of chocolate creams.

"I take it back. You aren't really a very smart junior sleuth, Dinah," Mrs. Chewbley said—and switched the cups. "Yours for mine. Did you honestly think I wouldn't guess what you were up to with that stupid spider remark? The old drugged-drink switcheroo is stale as last week's donuts."

Raising her cup to me, Mrs. Chewbley downed her tea all at once. "Now," she said, running her tongue over her lips to gather the last drops of the tea, "are you going to drink your tea and fall into a lovely, deep sleep, or do I call my associate?"

"What do you call him?" I joked nervously. I had to play for a bit of time. Just a bit. "Or maybe 'her,' if you mean Nurse Ballantyne. The 'he' is Bowl Cut, I assume."

Mrs. Chewbley shoved the still-full teacup at me with a pasty white fist. "Now drink up. I wouldn't want to have to force it down your throat, would I?" She started to rise.

"Fine." And I drank my tea, every last drop.

Chapter Twenty

Dinah Gets into the Vanishing Act

For a minute the only sound in the luggage car was the smooth hum of the Gold-and-Blue speeding along the tracks. Mrs. Chewbley and I eyeballed each other without blinking.

Then, finally, the piano teacher sagged back in her seat. A begrudging grin cracked her plump features. "You never switched the cups. I was wrong about you, Dinah Galloway. You *are* a smart—no, make that brainiac—junior sleuth. You've outwitted me fair and square. I've just downed the tea-dissolved sleeping pills I'd intended for you." She shook her head, and more hairpins cascaded.

I gulped. My impulse was to burst into tears of relief, but that could wait. I had to question Mrs. Chewbley while she was still conscious.

"You made Pantelli's piano teacher sick," I accused. "You

made Mr. Wellman sick—and you put something into my Coke yesterday in the dining car. No wonder you didn't want a taste of it when I offered! I thought I felt awfully queasy for just having taken a normal nap. Meanwhile, you calmly walked away to this hiding spot in the luggage car, where you already had," I gestured to the romance novels, "your reading material to help pass the long solitary hours."

Mrs. Chewbley shut her eyes. "I had to make you come and look for me, Dinah. Alone, without your oh-so-protective buddies. I thought I'd have to slip out in the dead of night to summon you in secret, but then, much more conveniently, you snooped your way here. And now I must ask you for the king. If *I* don't get it from you, my assistant will—and 'dead of night' will become more than just an expression. It'll be your epitaph."

"But I don't have—"

Loud, descending-the-scales-type yawn from Mrs. Chewbley. "Gracious, you've given us far more trouble about stealing back the king than we thought you would. A loudmouth twelve-year-old," Mrs. Chewbley marveled and opened an eyelid at me. "I could use a helper like you, Dinah. Ideal to train 'em young."

With a snore, she tipped forward. I grasped Mrs. Chewbley's shoulder and shoved her back into an upright position. "My goal is to sing at Carnegie Hall," I informed her, "not become the next Artful Dodger."

I heaved the dregs of both teacups at Mrs. Chewbley.

She spluttered awake. "Now, *talk*," I ordered. "What do you mean, steal the king back? Was he yours to begin with?"

Mrs. Chewbley giggled. "Sure he was—after I'd stolen him! Never mind from where, though. Thievers, keepers, I like to say. But then one night, just over seven years ago, my son was in a card game with Ardle McBean. The foolish boy ran out of money and offered the king up as an eighty-thousand-dollar bet. Ardle won the king—by *cheating*." Mrs. Chewbley tsked disapprovingly.

There was an irony in here somewhere, but I was too tired to pin it down. "Go on," I urged.

"Then Ardle, wanted by the police for a whole packet of break-ins and thefts, turned himself in and got slapped in jail for seven years. All that time I had to wait for my king—talk about your seven-year itch," Mrs. Chewbley sighed, and her eyelids began to flutter again. I gave her a not-too-friendly shake.

"Huh? Oh, right. Anyhow," she resumed, "I visited Ardle in jail, pestering him to tell me where the king was. I said we'd give him eighty grand." Here Mrs. Chewbley snorted. "The king's worth way more 'n that now, not that we told Ardle, of course.

"Finally, just before he got out of the slammer, Ardle admitted—spilled the McBeans, you might say—that he'd entrusted the king to your late dad. So I moved into your neighborhood to keep an eye on the Galloway household. I became the sweet, befuddled old lady fond of chocolate. *And I listened*. It's amazing what you find out if you listen.

Most people don't have that gift. I found out that Mrs. Grimsbottom taught piano. That among her students was a friend of yours, Pantelli Audia. That your mom thought it'd be good for you to take lessons too, from someone far more patient than sour Mrs. Grimsbottom.

"Whom, yes indeedy, I served horse-chestnut-spiked tea to. She grew violently ill, our Mrs. G."

Our Mrs. C. lapsed into a nostalgic, if sleepy, smile. "As did your agent, later on.

"Of course, I pretended not to know Ardle, and vice versa. It was part of the deal we were supposed to have. He gave me a start when he showed up at your window—I was afraid he'd tip you off to me! Like I say, you just can't trust that McBean.

"And then the stupid, soft-hearted man had a change of heart. Said he'd decided to be law-abiding, as he'd promised his late friend Mike Galloway. Ardle intended to retrieve the king from you and return it to its rightful owner! I knew I'd have to get the king from you myself—and silence Ardle before he blabbed to you." Mrs. Chewbley yawned. "Silence him...faster than a speeding Buick, shall we say?"

"Cut the jokes, Mrs. Chewbley," I said, unamused. The dissolved sleeping pills had relaxed the piano teacher into a would-be Ben Stiller. "Who *is* the rightful owner, anyway?"

"As to that," eyes shut, Mrs. Chewbley lolled around in her chair, "you'll have to find out yourself, Dinah Galloway."

With a sleepy shudder, the piano teacher fell face-first into an open box of chocolate creams.

I, however, was cured of any urge to snooze. My first thought: Scram in case Nurse Ballantyne shows up, with her baleful *wompf*!s and whispers.

Jumping up, I began to investigate the on-end trunk, which Mrs. Chewbley had claimed didn't open from the inside. Now that I knew she wasn't a kidnap victim, a prisoner, there was no reason to believe her.

But where *was* the exit? The trunk definitely didn't open from the inside. I heaved at it with my shoulder. Ow. Not smart, Dinah. That was my left shoulder, the one Nurse Ballantyne, in her guise as the Whisperer, kept wrenching out of its socket.

Never mind the Whisperer, whatever happened to Bowl Cut?

Deafening snore from Mrs. Chewbley. I guessed that was the only answer I could expect for the moment.

Massaging my shoulder, I leaned against the fabric-covered box to the left of the trunk.

And toppled backward. The box was hollow!

So that's how Mrs. Chewbley got in and out of her hiding place, I thought, gingerly picking myself up in the passageway. Well, at least now I could go for help.

I was about to propel my increasingly sore body toward the luggage-car door when it slid open to reveal a dark-trench-coated figure with hat pulled low. Even in the throes of poison ivy, Nurse Ballantyne couldn't resist gliding about menacingly.

I dove back into the box.

"Ma," Nurse Ballantyne hissed. Whoa. Mrs. Chewbley was Nurse Ballantyne's *mother*? This was the most charming mother-offspring match since Mrs. Bates and Norman.

Soft footsteps padded along the passageway. Any second the fabric would be thrust aside, and here she'd find me, stuck with the snoring Mrs. Chewbley.

I had to get out. But how? All those boxes, cartons and trunks loomed around me, hemming me in.

"*Ma.*"

The footsteps padded ever closer.

Sir Edmund Hillary I was not. As I frantically clawed my way up a stack of Lola's Lingerie boxes, one broke loose. Pink nightgowns slipped out, unfolding in mid-air to float down on Mrs. Chewbley. Soon her sleeping body was draped from head to toe.

I nearly toppled, but grabbed the edge of a wooden crate in time and heaved myself up. Below, I heard Nurse Ballantyne croak, in best Whisperer fashion, "What are you supposed to be, Ma, a giant strawberry sundae?"

Ah, a rare flash of humor from our poison-ivy-ravaged nurse. Strange—when not in Whisperer guise, Nurse Ballantyne never wisecracked.

Then the nurse erupted into an interesting assortment of whispered swear words—who said sleuthing wasn't a learning experience?

I also heard vicious slaps. Nurse Ballantyne was trying to rouse her maternal unit.

I crawled from the top of the carton to the top of Hans and Roman's giant, ebony, magic coffin. The top was slashed with painted-on lightning bolts. Nothing subtle about those guys.

Subtle. Now that's what *I* had to be. Subtle like a panther, I thought, inching forward in total silence. Hey, I wasn't doing too bad. Even Talbot, athletic and wiry as he was, couldn't be quieter than I was being.

With growing confidence, I inched along the top of the magic coffin. I leaned forward, putting my weight on my hands, and pitched headfirst into darkness.

Oh, that sinking feeling.

With a *smack*! I hit bottom.

But, no—it wasn't bottom, just a platform of some kind. Splintering noises, and I was falling again.

This time I landed on cushions, which would have been nice, except that the first body part to make contact was my much-damaged left shoulder. I let out a long howl of pain.

"That was helpful," remarked Pantelli in a laryngitic voice. "By crashing through that upper layer, you've gained us some light."

I raised one eyelid. The other was smushed into a cushion. Pantelli was right. From the very top, light was now dribbling down.

Across from me, Pantelli sat against a magic-coffin wall, calmly tucking back honey-roasted peanuts from a Gold-and-Blue snack bag.

He held out the bag to me. "Whenever Beanstalk, Freckles or some other conductor brings round the snack trays, I help myself to several of these at once," he explained. "You never know when you might need an extra shot of protein."

Conductors and snack trays...why did something flicker in my mind just then?

"That was a false bottom you cracked." Pantelli gestured up at the platform just above, now sporting a jagged-edged hole. He shook his head, marveling. "Always the dramatic entrances with you, Di."

Painfully I raised myself into a sitting position. I was wondering just how necessary to the rest of my life my left shoulder would be.

Wincing, I filled Pantelli in about finding Mrs. Chewbley— the new, definitely not improved Mrs. Chewbley. And about Nurse Ballantyne, a.k.a. the Whisperer, being close by.

"But how'd you end up in here?" I finished. "And did you see Talbot on your, er, travels?"

Pantelli shook his head. "I was too busy falling through a Hans and Roman trapdoor while you were staring at the woo-hoo cuckoo."

"A trapdoor at the base must be where their volunteers go in," I said. "Then Hans and Roman open the main part of the coffin, and the platform above hides the volunteer from the audience's view. Ver-r-ry tricky of Hans and Roman."

"Trickier still that there's no exit," Pantelli said glumly. "I tapped on, shoved at and, oh yeah, at one point *pleaded* with all four sides of this coffin thingy. As well as, natch, yelling my lungs hoarse. So, we're stuck.

"But hey," he pulled a card-sized box from a sweater pocket, "now that we've got some light, we can play Miniature Treevial Pursuit."

From the top of the coffin came a shrill whisper. "*Can I play?*"

Pantelli and I reacted less than suavely. We let out blood-curdling yells.

Above us, bony trousered legs swung through the opening—long, spindly feet dangled above us. The Whisperer was about to drop!

Pantelli and I each plastered ourselves against coffin walls to avoid being the Whisperer's bull's-eye. One of my knees struck something knobby. "Yeee-ouch" was my first reaction.

Then, frantically, it occurred to me that the knobby something might just be a latch. It *was*.

Above us, Nurse Ballantyne was flapping about like a flag. "Prepare to be flattened like two pancakes—*pest*-flavored pancakes," she hissed, with a dry, ominous chuckle.

I wrenched at the latch. Another trapdoor yawned open. Pantelli and I flopped through to land on the floor underneath. We let loose more yells.

Noise blared on and on. It took me a second to realize we weren't the sources of it anymore.

The opened latch had triggered Hans and Roman's built-in security alarm. A siren wailed.

Chapter Twenty-One

The Fisherman Resurfaces

Fzzzz! The stomach-remedy tablets dissolved. Head Conductor Wiggins drank deeply.

With Madge beside me, I'd confided everything, from my very first meeting at age five with Ardle, to Pantelli's and my scrambled escape from Nurse Ballantyne in the luggage car.

The head conductor examined his empty glass thoughtfully. He poured out fresh water from a glass pitcher and tossed two more tablets in.

Then he raised the fizzing glass to me. "I salute your health, Miss Galloway. As opposed to the tattered remains of my own health. You and your sister may be interested to learn that I've applied for early retirement. I'm a broken man, you see. *You've* broken me.

"But—it appears you were right about the vanishing

passenger." Head Conductor Wiggins gave a rather high-pitched laugh. "Passen*gers*, I should say! Why *me*, I sometimes wonder? No, no, it doesn't matter." He sighed.

As assistant head conductor, Beanstalk was now in the luggage car, trying to wake Mrs. Chewbley up for questioning. The police in Toronto were also waiting to question her.

The other conductors were combing the train cars for Talbot. The protests of passengers woken up for a second night in a row, as conductors checked their compartments, pierced the office door like darts.

With Head Conductor Wiggins busy staring into his stomach-remedy liquid, my sister turned to me. She'd started out by giving me bear hugs, but now we were into scolding.

"Why didn't you tell Mother and me about this 'king' business? And to remove that envelope of Dad's without saying anything—well, that's just unforgivable. It's her final memento of him."

This was the tough part. "It was for Ardle's sake," I began—but I couldn't figure out the words to explain that I kind of liked Ardle. Just as I would always like people whose outside roughness hid an inside goodness. Or semi-goodness, anyway. Madge and Talbot, I realized, didn't have time for the Ardles of the world. Not that I liked Madge and Talbot any less for that. It was just the way they were. But Dad had found time for the Ardles, and, now, so did I. They made life more interesting. Maybe it was the challenge of trying to find the goodness—okay, semi-goodness—in them.

Nor could I explain my feeling to Madge that, somehow, Dad wanted me to unearth the mysterious king and set things right for Ardle.

I was too worried about Talbot to mind being scolded. Where *was* Talbot? Nurse Ballantyne was claiming not to know, and Mrs. Chewbley still snored happily in the luggage car.

Freddy stuck his freckled nose in. "Nurse Ballantyne's agreed to be questioned by you, sir," he announced. "Not *cheerfully* agreed, mind," he added and rolled his eyes.

"We don't need on-the-spot commentary, McClusky," the head conductor frowned. "When will you learn that a conductor's role is to be quiet and discreet?"

Freddy held up his hands in surrender. "Sorr-ee." He pushed the door open, revealing Nurse Ballantyne swathed in a white fleecy robe, her splotchy, poison-ivy-infected face jutting out of it like a rutabaga. Freddy said, "C'mon in, Nurse Ballantyne. Er—no offence, ma'am, but don't brush up against anyone. We don't want your, y'know, your," he lowered his voice, "PI."

Wompf! Nurse Ballantyne flattened him against the wall. "'PI' got me into this all right," she glowered, striding into the room. She thrust a long, bony finger at me. "This underage *private investigator*!"

Head Conductor Wiggins drained the last of his stomach-remedy drink. "You must admit, Nurse Ballantyne," he said, dabbing at his mouth with a gold-bordered blue napkin, "that Dinah has proved to be correct. Edwina Chewbley did disappear, though of her own will, rather than as a kidnap victim. Mrs. Chewbley believes Dinah has a valuable stamp. You do too, don't you, Nurse? Isn't that why you grabbed Dinah's purse at the Forks Market—*not realizing it was full of poison ivy?* In fact, you're the Whisperer, are you not?"

Nurse Ballantyne spat back, "I found that purse on my desk. I opened it to find out who the owner was. Obviously I was set up." Pulling a bottle of calamine lotion from her robe pocket, she began splashing its contents agitatedly over her face, neck and arms.

Madge leveled one of her glacial blue gazes at the nurse. "Someone has been stalking my sister, Nurse Ballantyne. Right now, you have the doubtful distinction of being the number one suspect."

"Hmph!" Nurse Ballantyne shook out more lotion. She caught me staring at her hand as she did so. "Well," she barked, "what do you want now?"

"Nothing," I said. But it had come back again: that vague sense, prompted by something Pantelli had said in the Hans and Roman magic coffin, that I had missed an important clue.

But where *was* Talbot? *Where WAS he, where WAS he*, beat the wheels of the train, skimming smoothly along their tracks.

Madge told me to wait outside the office while, over the speakerphone, she and Head Conductor Wiggins talked to the Royal Canadian Mounted Police. "The Mounties should be asking *me* the questions," I'd objected. Madge assured me they would, all in good time. They wanted to speak to the adults first, she explained. "The trademark Dinah Galloway melodramatic version comes later, when they've had a chance to prepare themselves with some aspirin."

Freddy, passing by just then, winked at me, but he and the other porters were too busy to chat. To make up for everyone's compartment being searched yet again for yet another missing passenger, Head Conductor Wiggins had ordered early-morning treats for everyone. The porters were wheeling carts of refreshments from compartment to compartment.

Doors opened at the porters' knocks; sleepy faces in halos of mussed hair glared out.

"Coffee or tea?" Freddy asked.

"Anything but Dinah Galloway," a woman snapped, grabbed a pot of coffee and several muffins, and slammed her door.

Boy, was I unpopular. Would an unpopular singer ever be invited to sing at Crumbly Hall? "Carnegie," I corrected myself and uttered a huge sigh. I trudged along the passageway, feeling useless and very sorry for myself.

Where WAS he, where WAS he...

The anxious refrain kept on, and all the time more doors were opening, more glares volleying out.

Almost at the end of the car, yet another door opened; another passenger appeared. I summoned my best scowl.

And got a lazy smile in return. The man with the pointed beard—the fisherman! Only this time he wore a red-tasseled nightcap instead of a tweedy, tackle-decorated fisherman's hat, and red-and-white-striped pj's instead of denim shirt and shorts.

"I didn't know you were on board," I blurted out.

He shrugged, causing the red tassel to flip about. "I can blend into a crowd very easily. Did you ever find your king, Dinah?"

"No," I said. "I had the wrong king all along. It's not Charles the First I'm looking for, but Edward the Eighth."

The fisherman's smile broadened. He seemed pleased, as if I were a student of his who had just aced an exam. "If you know the *who*, the *where* may follow, like daffodils after February rain."

All at once my patience, which I didn't have great quantities of at the best of times, disappeared—another vanishing passenger, you might say. I'd had enough of mysterious utterances. Enough of everything.

"You're so smart, you answer your own questions," I snapped at him. "Am I the one who kidnaps people and steals valuable stamps? No-o-o-o. But guess who everybody dumps on—yours miserably truly."

Still looking irritatingly good-humored, the fisherman tapped his chin. "There's a song in that, I believe. At last, an improvement on that 'Black Socks' ditty you've been belting out."

"What, you're a music critic now?"

But he'd stepped away from the door. I heard a couple of clicks; then the volume was turned up. An instrumental version of an old standard floated into the passageway.

The fisherman called, "Know this one, Dinah?"

"Of course," I said, frowning at him. This seemed an odd time to play Name That Tune. "It's 'Nobody's Baby.' Dad used to pound it out for me on our ancient piano. He said most singers cooed the tune, but I should go full throttle on it."

The fisherman reached in to crank up the volume. "Sing now," he suggested. "You need to think. Where's Talbot? Where's the stamp? People think best when they're in a creative mood, which in your case involves making lots of noise."

I gaped at him. But he was right. I did have to think.

I'm nobody's baby

I wonder why...

I rocked and rollicked the song. Compartment doors reopened. This time, though, the sleepy, cross faces were breaking into grudging smiles.

But where *was* Talbot?

On the walkie-talkie, Talbot had warned me to get out of the luggage car. Because that's where he'd been captured, and he didn't want *me* to be. And because that's where he was being held.

Or so I'd assumed.

Nobody wants me,

I'm blue somehow...

Ryan sidled out of his compartment, and I took his hand. Pausing in my song for a moment, I whispered, "I'm like you. I love to sing, but smooth-talking like Edward the Eighth? Forget it!"

Ryan beamed. I resumed singing—and thinking.

With all its cartons and trunks, the luggage car was the perfect place to stash someone. Mrs. Chewbley had hidden there. Pantelli had fallen into Hans and Roman's magic coffin there.

On the walkie-talkie, Talbot had said he was "in with the dolls." But I'd already noticed those doll cartons weren't big enough to hold anyone much bigger than my cat Wilfred. Maybe Talbot was *behind* the doll cartons.

If only that stupid cuckoo hadn't been *woo-hoo*-ing overhead! I could have heard Talbot better.

Won't someone hear my plea...

The fisherman was beaming at me. Passengers were crowding every doorway now. One lady was smiling and dabbing at her eyes with a gold-edged blue facecloth. Everybody felt like nobody's baby sometimes, I realized. My dad had made me feel like that when he went and got himself killed from drinking too much.

Then—it wasn't the CD I was singing along with anymore, but Dad, beside me, bashing out the notes on our old piano.

And take a chance with me...

Dad said, *Take a chance on yourself, Dinah. Know what you know.*

What do I know? I asked him silently while holding one of my Methuselah's-lifetime-long notes. *Okay. I know that, between walkie-talkie crackles, Talbot asked for my help, while overhead, that stupid cuckoo...*

Abruptly I stopped singing. The cuckoo had been *woo-hoo*-ing overhead. *But not on the other end of the walkie-talkie.*

Talbot couldn't possibly be in the luggage car.

Chapter Twenty-Two

She Might Have Gnome

Dolls, Talbot had said. But maybe I'd heard "dolls" because of the power of suggestion. The boxes of Petrie's Porcelain Dolls were looming in front of me.

What else could Talbot have meant?

Know what you know.

The other passengers were applauding. Dad, at the piano, grinned at me and started fading.

I glared at him. "You have a definite Cheshire cat quality to you."

What? You're giving lip to a ghost?

Amid the applause, the fisherman cupped his ear at me. "What was that about cats, Dinah?"

"Uh, nothing." I managed a fake bared-teeth smile. "Y'know, *Cats*. Great musical." I raised my voice over the applause. "Listen, thanks, everyone. I just want to say that I'm really sorry about all the disruptions on this trip. Disappearing passengers, sleep deprivation and all that."

"It's all right, dear," the weepy woman called. "It's rather like being on one of those mind-and-body-toughening Outward Bound treks. Rock climbing, muddy river fording—except that, in place of those, we have you." She dabbed at her eyes some more.

"Thanks," I said, a bit doubtfully.

And stared at her. Specifically at the gold and blue facecloth she was drenching with her tears.

Pantelli had used one of those to mop his forehead when he, Talbot and I were hatching investigative plans in the linen closet. Among the towels.

Towels, Talbot had said. Not *dolls*.

"Um," I said loudly. But the passengers were all chatting about my powerful singing voice.

"A knock 'em dead voice."

"Thrilling—although her fondness for late-night commotion is unsettling."

"Oh well, these show-biz folk. Always slightly off, if you know what I mean."

Only the fisherman stood apart, with his sleepy smile. I paced up to him. "Mr.—who are you, anyway?"

"Jonathan Hector," he returned lazily. "Hector the Protector, they call me."

Brother, I thought. And people think *I'm* slightly off. "Uh, oka-a-ay. But for now, Talbot's in the linen supply room, probably a prisoner, and I'm going to spring him."

~ ~ ~

I wrenched open the linen-supply-room door. From down the corridor, in the infirmary, Nurse Ballantyne spotted me. She was applying a sponge drenched in calamine lotion to her forehead. Her nose, down which drops of the lotion were speeding like a mountain stream, quivered in fury. She stuck her right foot out and slammed the infirmary door shut.

Something about Beverly Ballantyne nagged at me, something all mixed up with the image of Pantelli chomping peanuts in Hans and Roman's magic coffin.

But I couldn't think about that now. I stepped into the linen supply room.

"Talbot?" I peered round at the stacks of plump navy towels. "Talbot?" I said louder. No response.

I began pulling towels off their stacks, pawing through them in case Talbot was underneath. Soon towels were toppling all around me.

Oof—some on top of me, as well. Was it possible to drown in terrycloth? I struggled to stay above them. "TALBOT!!!"

Then, from the far wall, a thud.

The towels were avalanching on me now. Some buried me; I fought my way up again.

Thud. Straightening my glasses, I squinted over the sea of navy towels. The hamper. The giant one I'd sat on top of and kicked my heels against.

Those thuds were kicks. And given the five LARGER THAN LIFE! SOLID STONE! garden gnomes piled on the lid, the kicks were signals for help, not a lively two-step.

Flailing, I tobogganed down a towel stack to ram right into the hamper. I heard a muffled *owwww*.

"Sorry," I called and heaved the garden gnomes off the lid, one by one.

Talbot was at the bottom of the hamper, compacted like a tinned sardine under the weight of towels. Unable to move, he hadn't been able to yell out, either—his mouth had been duct-taped shut.

R-r-rip! He peeled the tape off in one painful gesture that left the lower part of his face resembling an oversized stick of cinnamon gum.

"Ouch," I said for him, since he needed a minute to gasp in big breaths of air. I quickly filled him in on the latest developments. "So," I finished, "Mrs. Chewbley's unconscious and Nurse Ballantyne's more or less confined to the infirmary."

"A normal day in the life of Dinah Galloway, in other words."

"And what happened to *you?*"

Talbot grimaced. "While Pantelli, way down the aisle from me, pored over his leaves, I noticed that what I'd thought was a box covered with hanging fabric was just— hanging fabric. I started to push through when *wompf!* A fist descended on the top of my head."

"That would have been Nurse Ballantyne, stopping you before you could discover Mrs. Chewbley," I said grimly.

"The Whis—I mean, Nurse Ballantyne then threw a laundry bag over my head, tightened the strings around my neck and whispered, 'It's not much to ask is it, buddy-o? The stamp. I WANT THE STAMP.' To which I said, 'Why don't you just use e-mail?'"

"And you got an appreciative whisper-laugh?"

"I got another *wompf!* 'The stamp. Such a little thing to ask for. Well, let's see if I can't change your mind.' She whispered that if I didn't want Pantelli to disappear as well, I'd better go quietly with her.

"Nurse Ballantyne dragged me, half-stumbling because my head ached and I couldn't see, through car after car. She hissed, 'For your tree-freak buddy's sake, if anyone stops us, stay limp. Nobody'll recognize me with this hat pulled low. I'll pretend to be a passenger with laundry. And *you're* the laundry, get it? So method-act for me, kid.' She snorted at her, uh, humor.

"Finally Nurse Ballantyne stuffed me in this hamper, and then she left for a few minutes to get duct tape. That's when I got a few words out to you on the walkie-talkie."

Talbot rubbed his chin. "Hey, nice singing by the way. That's what gave me the energy to apply running shoe to hamper."

He held my hand. We grinned at each other for a long moment that, when I was younger, like a few days earlier, I would've described as soppy. And all at once I didn't mind anymore the knowing, older-sisterly looks Madge sometimes gave me about Talbot.

We got up and slip-slid across the towels. Near the door, Talbot swayed wildly. Unusual for someone so well-coordinated, was my first thought. Then I realized he was holding the left side of his head. A purple lump was emerging—a souvenir of Nurse Ballantyne's fist.

"We have to get you to a first-aid kit," I said.

"One wielded by Nurse Frankenstein? Yeah, sure. I might as well check into a funeral home right now."

"Madge has a first-aid kit," I informed him as he stumbled out into the passageway. I took his arm. "Look on the bright side. The lump on your head matches your shiner."

Unamused, Talbot mumbled something about taking out insurance on himself next time he went anywhere with me. I was too distracted to be insulted—I'd just realized that I felt strangely light and unburdened.

The unwieldy walkie-talkie! I must've dropped it while scrambling through the towels.

"You go ahead. I'll be right with you," I promised Talbot and scooted back into the linen supply room.

Chapter Twenty-Three

The Secret of Black Socks

The walkie-talkie lay broken, a coil still bouncing from inside it, on a patch of floor between two Tower of Pisa-like towel stacks. I picked it up carefully. Phew! Anyone finding it would have chucked it into the nearest wastebasket.

And I'd encouraged the idea of the walkie-talkie as junk by loudly making fun of it and leaving it jutting out of my pocket at all times so that anyone could have swiped it. Which meant no one had wanted to...

Sitting down on one of the less wobbly towel mountains, I pried apart the two sides of the walkie-talkie. Talbot's invention might not have won any beauty prizes at a tech convention, but it had worked when needed. Thanks to the walkie-talkie, he'd been able to signal me from the bottom of the hamper.

And thanks to the walkie-talkie, I'd had the perfect place

to hide Dad's envelope. I slid it out now from behind a battery and some wires.

Not that the envelope was valuable. I knew that now. It might have *once* contained the King Edward the Eighth stamp. Dad, or someone else, had long ago removed it.

The stamp. Such a little thing to ask for, Nurse Ballantyne had whispered to Talbot.

A little thing...

The King Eddie had been smaller than a lot of stamps now. The Forks Market stamp seller had remarked on how, back in the 1930s, there were no big colorful stamps.

I tipped the envelope back and forth, watching the light catch on the elk's golden flanks here, the purple of the background mountains there. A big beautiful stamp. Set an old small stamp near it and you'd hardly notice the old one.

Hardly notice...

I was five years old again, tugging at Dad's hand as, in amusement and exasperation, he shooed Ardle McBean off our porch.

Dad demanded, "You know the dangers of secondhand smoke to a kid?" He pushed me behind him again; I popped right out, like a jack-in-the-box.

Ardle laugh-coughed. "Okay, I'll git. I just wanted to make sure the king was okay, that's all. Guess you don't want to talk about the king in front o' the kid, though."

He gestured at me with his cigarette, scattering ashes

over the porch Mother had just swept. "That sure is some
songbird you got there, Mike. She makes 'Black Socks'
sound like a Broadway show."

Dad grinned at me. "How do the lyrics to that go?" he
teased and crooned:

Dinah's socks,

That she never washes,

You'd hardly notice

One from the next.

"No, no!" I exclaimed, jumping up and down. "Not
like that, Dad."

But Dad was narrowing his eyes at Ardle. "The king
is safe, okay? Hidden, so no one will find him. We clear
on that?"

"Yeah, we're clear," Ardle said...

Clear on what? I wondered, tipping the elk back and forth
some more. Dad hadn't actually told Ardle where the king
stamp was.

Or had he?

"Black Socks" had been going through my mind since
Ardle's return. As if taunting me to understand the secret it
held. Except that I'd been singing the correct "Black Socks"
lyrics. Maybe, all the time, the secret had been in the lyrics
Dad made up: *You'd hardly notice one from the next.*

And then, at last, I got it.

I was already prying the elk stamp off the envelope.
Dad had only wet the back of the elk stamp at the edges. I

peeled it off, and there, underneath, in shrink-wrap, rested the purple coronation stamp that had been too hastily printed for a king who never claimed his crown.

"Long live the king," remarked a comfortable voice in front of me.

My heart did one of those horrible pole-vaulting routines. The fisherman stood before me, arms folded and a satisfied smile playing above his pointed beard. He now wore a pinstripe jacket over his pajamas.

"Bravo," he said. "I wonder if I might have the stamp now?"

"No," I said, annoyed. I might have known *he'd* be after the stamp too. Everyone else was. "Why don't you take up, say, coin collecting?"

I stepped to one side to bypass the fisherman. He blocked me. "Okay," I said. "Here. Take it." I held out the envelope.

But before he could grab it, I whipped my hand up to the tassel of his nightcap. I gave a good tug.

"Bowl Cut!" I shouted. I dodged round him, unfortunately sliding to fall on some towels. Avoiding his outstretched hand, I crawled away. "That pointed beard," I panted. "Very cunning. Hides the dinner-plate shape of your face."

Bowl Cut looked rather hurt. "Listen, I've never pretended to be Brad Pitt," he puffed. "And I have this bowl cut for an upcoming Roundhead-versus-Cavaliers battle—" He fell backward; towels piled on top of him.

I was almost at the supply room door. "I thought *I* had a problem with lateness," I tossed back. "For your information, the Battle of Worcester happened more than three hundred and fifty years ago."

The door jolted open. Just a crack, because of the fallen towels wedged against it, but enough to knock me backward.

Freddy's freckled face peered in, his eyes big and round over his turned-up nose as he surveyed the sea of navy towels. "What is this, the set of *Titanic*?" Shoving hard, he managed to move the towels enough to squeeze in.

He reached out to help me up.

"Am I glad you're here!" I said. "I finally found the stamp, and this guy's trying to grab it from me." I gestured at Bowl Cut, who was cartwheeling his arms in an effort to stand up straight as he plowed toward us.

"Huh," Freddy scowled. "I'll take care of *him*." Grabbing one of the walkie-talkie halves from me, he hurled it at Bowl Cut. *Bam!* Down Bowl Cut went, clutching his forehead and moaning. *Bam!* Freddy winged the other half, and Bowl Cut sank onto the towels.

So now Talbot's invention had served three uses: communication, hiding place and scud missile. I objected, "I'm not sure if it was necessary to—"

Freddy interrupted, "Let's see this ker-*ayz*ee stamp that's been causing so much trouble." He held out his hand.

It was gloved.

And it was his *left* hand.

Then I knew what had bothered me when Pantelli was dive-bombing peanuts into his mouth in Hans and Roman's magic coffin. *Whenever Beanstalk, Freckles or some other conductor brings round the snack trays, I help myself to several of these at once*, he'd explained. And I'd thought of Freddy offering treat baskets to passengers.

With his left hand.

When the Whisperer threw the blanket over me, a non-visual sense had kicked in after all—only not the sense of hearing or smell, as I'd expected. The sense of *feeling*. The shoulder that the Whisperer wrenched and bruised was my left one, which only a left-handed person would reach for. Nurse Ballantyne couldn't possibly be the Whisperer. I'd watched her repeatedly splash on the calamine lotion with her *right* hand. She'd been telling the truth. Somebody, a prudently gloved somebody, had booby-trapped her by leaving the poison-ivy-filled purse on her desk.

Was Freddy—nice, friendly, freckled Freddy—that somebody? Was he the Whisperer?

I raised a hand to my mouth and uttered what was probably the phoniest cough in history. "Kinda stuffy in here, isn't it? Maybe I'll just pop outside and—"

Freddy twisted my elbow. "Nothin' doin'. You're gonna give me that stamp." He lunged for my other hand, the one that gripped the envelope. I stretched my arm as far as I could. I also plunged my teeth into his wrist, what you might call multitasking.

"YEEOOWW." Cursing, Freddy dragged me to the wall. "I knew Ma was being too soft with you. 'We'll join our little songbird sleuth on the Gold-and-Blue,' Ma said. 'Me *and* you, cuz there's a midnight job for a conductor open,' she said. 'We'll wait for the right opportunity to grab the stamp.'

"Ha! 'Grab the kid and you'll get the stamp,' I told Ma."

"You're her son," I said between winces at the pain he was causing my elbow. "You're also the Whisperer. I heard you hissing for your 'Ma,' except that I thought you were Nurse Ballantyne. I'll have to buy out the entire stock of FTD to make up the insult to her."

"Yeah, wiseacre warbler, I'm Ma's son by her first marriage. So whoop-dee-doo. The *stamp*, kid."

"Why?" I taunted him, playing for time since I didn't know what else to do. "You're not very reliable with it. You lost it to Ardle in a card game."

"What is this, gloat-at-the-Fredster time?" Freddy punched over a stack of towels. Daylight flooded the linen supply room from a window beyond. He shoved till the window slid open.

I wrenched and pulled, struggling to break from Freddy's clamp-like hold. No dice. He bundled me up and onto the sill.

And over. I dug my heels in below the windowsill. They, and Freddy's grip on my left hand, were all that kept me from flying *splat*! into the blurry green of the field below.

"The stamp!" growled Freddy between gritted teeth. His face was stretched so tight with rage that his freckles looked ready to spring off.

I fluttered, kite-like, in the wind. My loved ones fluttered before me too: Mother, Madge, Jack, Wilfred the cat...my best buddies, Talbot and Pantelli...The train rounded a curve and *smash*—the wind flattened me against the side of the train. If I fell, the wind might flatten me up against those churning wheels. Let's see. The blender setting would be *chop*, I believe.

"THE STAMP!" Freddy yelled. He loosened his hold slightly.

"AAAGGGHHH!" I screamed and threw up. We were going so fast that the barf flew sideways, not down. Memo to self, possibly the last: There's nothing glamorous about being a damsel in distress.

From behind Freddy, a yell: "WOMPF!"

Having clambered up a towel stack, Ryan whipped a rolled-up towel down hard on Freddy's head. "WOMPF!" Freddy fell, pulling me in enough so that I was able to angle my arm inside the window and press it against the wall. I shifted my weight over the sill. Just a bit more...

Freddy struggled up, started to push me out again. My loved ones re-flashed before me. Including Dad this time.

Dad winked at me. *Remember—you'll sing one day at Carnegie Hall.*

"I WILL!" I shouted with all I'd got. After all, these could be my last words.

Freddy tightened his clench on my fingers, reeled me in. "You will? You'll give me the stamp?"

"YES!"

Freddy yanked me back up on the windowsill. "Gimme." He reached for the envelope, which I still waved in the air.

"SURE!" I yelled. "Here, it's all yours"—and I let the envelope go.

With a frenzied howl, Freddy lunged after it.

And toppled out the window.

Ryan helped me in. Hugging each other, we watched Freddy bounce on the grass beside the tracks, roll down a slope and into a blackberry patch. A second howl echoed back to us.

"I'LL GET MR. WIGGINS TO SEND HELP," I bellowed.

I received a grunt in reply. Except that the grunt came from behind us. Bowl Cut, the left side of his head bloodied, was dragging himself painfully across the towels. Weakly, he struggled to standing position and swayed back and forth for a moment before speaking. "Interesting way to dispose of villains, Dinah. Chuck them from moving vehicles."

"I didn't! I was just—"

But then Bowl Cut, very pale, began to pitch forward. I grabbed his arm. "You need Madge's first-aid kit. Under normal circumstances, I'd take you to the infirmary, but Nurse Ballantyne's infected with poison ivy. Besides," I added, helping him past a mountain of towels, "I'd better not see Nurse Ballantyne again till I have a fully rehearsed, minimum-two-hour apology ready for all the trouble I've caused her."

"With you around, there are no normal circumstances," Bowl Cut said, with the ghost of a smile. "But before I pass out, perhaps I should properly introduce myself." He handed me a business card.

"'Jonathan Hector, Hector the Protector Insurance,'" I read. "'Specializing in insurance for historical valuables.'" I put the card down and stared at him. "Valuables such as...stamps?"

Jonathan Hector nodded. "I got into insurance of artifacts, of historical treasures, because history's my passion. Seven years ago, the King Edward the Eighth 'blooper stamp,' as it's called, was stolen from Vancouver's Monarchy Forever! Museum. The stamp had been insured with my company for eighty thousand dollars. Sensing that the few existing copies of the blooper stamp would hugely increase in value, the museum's directors asked me to track down the stamp rather than pay them out the eighty grand. No matter how long it took, they said—and they'd finance my investigations."

Jonathan pressed a hand towel against his head. "I found out that one Edwina Chewbley, with a record of petty thefts, had been a Monarchy Forever! Museum volunteer at the time the King Eddie disappeared. Seems Mrs. Chewbley was so sweet and dithering that no one worried about letting her hang around the exhibits unsupervised. She left the museum soon after the stamp disappeared.

"Then our friendly local card shark, Ardle McBean, won the stamp off Freddy. Fast-forward seven years. As soon as Ardle got out of prison, I approached him about returning the stamp. He was leery at first, but was starting to come round to do the right thing—and then Freddy ran him over. I tried to grab Ardle from the back, but too late."

I shook my head, bewildered. "In Garden Park, when I got to Ardle, I thought he was pointing accusingly at you. But he was pointing at Freddy, vrooming away in the dented Buick. And you..."

"I was checking Ardle's heart rate," Jonathan explained. "Ardle's eyes flickered open. He mumbled, 'Watch over Mike Galloway's kid...' I promised him I would.

"Once I realized someone was calling nine-one-one for him, I got out of there. If the police found and questioned me, I'd have had to tell them the truth, and my cover would've been wrecked. Better, I thought, to quietly shadow you so I could both protect you and keep tracking down the stamp. I figured you must know where it was—without knowing you knew."

"So many shadows," I sighed. "Shadows—friendly and otherwise—hovering around me. And," I added sadly, "shadows from the past."

"Those past shadows are the ones we all have with us, in one form or another," Jonathan replied kindly. "That's why we have passions in life, you with singing, me with history—to chase them away."

We reached the door, and Jonathan stretched out a hand to the knob, as much to steady himself as to turn it. "I'm sorry I had to be so mysterious with you, Dinah. You know, rudely reaching through your kitchen window without explanation. And then my fisherman disguise, not to mention my endlessly cryptic remarks. It was part of my agreement with the Monarchy Forever! Museum. The directors feared that if anyone discovered I was after the King Edward stamp, all the collectors on the continent would descend like crows to an open garbage bag. The directors ordered me to stay mum no matter what.

"Also, I didn't want Ma Chewbley and her son to recognize me from seven years ago, when I'd been asking questions about the stamp. I knew from her screech she'd recognized me at your house that day. Hence my fisherman's disguise. And the need to keep out of sight on the Gold-and-Blue till absolutely necessary."

"Mrs. Chewbley claimed she saw you boarding the Gold-and-Blue in Jasper," I said thoughtfully. "But she described you as Bowl Cut, which you weren't, in fisherman mode. I bet she was making that up so I'd trust her."

"No doubt. That sweet, dithery routine of Edwina's goes a long way. Oh, and my bowl-cut hairdo—not my regular look, I assure you. I'm appearing in a minor role as a Roundhead in a historical film I'm insuring called *Roundheads, Cavaliers and Werner the Talking Dog*."

"So that's the battle you meant," I said. "A movie one." I

tried to look excited for him, but privately I found Werner the Talking Dog movies silly. So much *barking*.

Jonathan sighed and twisted the knob, holding the door open for me. "All this trouble, and now the stamp's gone, lost in a southern Ontario field of blue corn."

In response I stuck out my tongue at him.

Chapter Twenty-Four

The Best King of All

Toronto! Pantelli, Talbot and I craned out the window to see the CN Tower. At one thousand, eight hundred and fifteen feet high, the Tower is the world's tallest freestanding structure.

We agreed that the Tower resembled a long ballpoint pen with a hula hoop about two-thirds of the way up. Part of the hoop was actually the observation deck, with a floor made of glass. Awesome. We all intended to take barf bags up.

Laugh-cough from the other end of the cell phone I was holding. I'd been describing the tower to Ardle, who'd recovered enough to sit up in his hospital bed.

"Don't talk about barfin', Miss Carnegie Hall," he begged. "I bin through enough o' that after unsteady Freddy pancaked me with his Buick. Hey, you say the stamp is safe?"

"It was safe all along. When Freddy yelled at me to hand it over, I faked a cough and stuck it under my tongue."

"Whoa, Nellie! Mike 'ud be proud o' ya. *I'm* proud o' ya. Heck, you'd be a great con artist, Miss Carnegie Hall. Why, you an' I could—"

"Never mind, Ardle," I said disapprovingly. What was it with people trying to recruit me to the underworld all of a sudden? "Besides, Jonathan says he has a job waiting for you—as a security guard. On the theory that it takes a thief to catch a thief, you'd be ideal at knowing when valuables, in a museum, say, are in danger."

"A *museum*?" echoed Ardle, horrified. "What a rotten way fer a guy to become honest. Though, I gotta say, it can't be as tough as cuttin' out smokes has bin."

"I'm not sympathizing with you about that," I said firmly. "It's time you stopped resembling Pigpen."

To someone beside him, Ardle protested, "Aw, lady, not orange juice...I tell ya, this healthy, moral livin' 'ull be the end o' old Ardle."

Mother came on. Let's just say her voice was not fraught with good humor. "Dinah, before I list the many, *many* things you've done to deserve a lifetime's grounding, I want to know who Calvin Blimburg is."

"Calvin—? He phoned *you*?" I clapped my hand to my head. I must've given the mysterious Calvin our home number instead of Madge's cell one.

"Yes, this Mr. Blimburg is a counselor with Alcoholics Anonymous. He helps people get rid of their addiction problem. He said you left a strange, threatening message on his voice mail."

"Oh, wow. Oh, wow." I shut my eyes and felt tears oozing out from between the lids. Dad had been phoning AA. He'd been seeking help.

Mother wailed, "Dinah, I was so embarrassed! I can't have you phoning strangers and—"

"Mother," I gulped, "I love you so much. I have something really nice to tell you about Dad, but I want to wait till I see you. Will that be okay?"

"Something nice about—Mike?" Mother's voice became young and warm, the way it must've sounded when she and Dad sat in their Commercial Drive café, talking about the possibilities ahead of them. "Well...all right. Yes, that'll be okay."

The Gold-and-Blue slid into the city. Talbot told me more about Edward the Eighth and what happened after he quit his throne.

I was still thinking about this when, on exiting the train, I collided with Madge.

"*Ow*, Dinah!"

On the Union Station platform, porters jostled to help Madge down.

"Here, allow *me*, miss!"

"No, allow *me*—to give you a hand and my life's devotion."

At the next set of train doors down from us, a beaming ,head-bandaged Jonathan Hector appeared, with a small steel briefcase chained to his wrist. Inside: the King Edward the Eighth stamp.

Three armed guards, with *Hector The Protector Insurance* in bold red letters on the backs of their white uniforms, were waiting at the bottom of the stairs for Jonathan.

I waved at him. "I told Ardle about the security guard job," I called. "He was—well, mildly enthusiastic."

"There might be a job for you too, Dinah. A singing role in *Cavaliers, Roundheads and Werner the Talking Dog*. I'll speak to the director about it."

"But didn't you say they're about to start filming?" I yelled back. "It might be a little late to—"

"Not when you consider that I'm giving them a special discount on their insurance." Jonathan was winking. Then he stepped down to join the guards, and they moved off in the crowd.

I prodded Madge in the back. "There are fire regulations about blocking exits." Suitcase-laden people were crowding up behind me, including Talbot with his guitar and Pantelli with his toilet-paper box full of leaf samples.

With a haughty sniff, Madge permitted herself to be helped down to the platform. I peered round to see why she'd hesitated for so long.

Jack!

He stood glaring at her. She was glaring back. Ah, I thought. A showdown over the other woman, Veronica LaFlamme.

The *way* he was glaring at Madge, though. It was a mixture of exasperation—and utter adoration. A tiny doubt entered my mind. Could I have been wrong? But no, those e-mails spoke for themselves.

Jack shouted at Madge, "What's the idea, telling me our engagement's off? Since I got your phone message, I haven't been able to work, eat or sleep. I changed my flight to a red-eye just so I could arrive early at this station and *pace*. In fact, I'm ready to start pulling pillars down with my bare hands just so I can make my pacing path clearer."

"What a disturbed young man," a woman murmured behind me. "It wasn't bad enough that *barf* hurled through my window at me early this morning, just when I was trying to snap a picture of blue corn!" She hurried past Jack.

Madge replied to Jack with cold dignity, "I *tried* to reach you, Jack. But you were always unavailable. With that LaFlamme woman, I suppose."

Jack looked bewildered. "I was deep in a forest, out of e-mail range, with a conservationist group. We were trying to track down a possible spotted owl sighting. The one time you got through to me by cell, the connection broke."

Then Jack paused, rewinding her comments. "The 'LaFlamme woman'? *Veronica* LaFlamme?"

"I see you've conveniently remembered," Madge returned. Her eyes brightened with tears. So he wasn't even denying it! On Madge's behalf, I scowled at him.

Talbot and Pantelli waited on either side of me. I could see Talbot was uncomfortable being in on a private quarrel.

I didn't have to glance at Pantelli to know *his* reaction: delight. He came from a big family whose members were always arguing—and enjoying themselves hugely while at it.

Pantelli now inquired cheerfully of Madge and Jack, "You two breaking up?" Setting down his suitcase and leaf-sample box, he began shot-putting peanuts into his mouth.

Jack stepped closer to Madge and proceeded to glare eyeball-to-eyeball at her. "Do you know who Veronica LaFlamme is, Madge? *Do* you? Here." And out of his back jeans pocket he withdrew a folded-up newspaper. "I was planning to ask you about this civilly, over lunch, away from," he cast a foul glance at Pantelli, "the small-fry set."

He unfolded the newspaper, the previous day's *Vancouver Sun*. A photo of Jack was on the front; beside him beamed a short, fat, middle-aged woman with corkscrew curls. Underneath, the headline *Head of Environmental Party Asks Young Activist to Run for City Council in November Elections*.

My tiny doubt ballooned to whale size. "Uh-oh," I murmured to Talbot and Pantelli.

"*That's* Veronica LaFlamme?" Madge squeaked. "And those secret meetings you were having with her—the news that you were going to break to me—"

Jack placed his hands on her shoulders and regarded her solemnly. "I wouldn't agree to run for council unless it was okay with you, Madge. It'll make our lives even busier at a time when we're still in school and about to get married, besides."

Tears were spilling from Madge's blue eyes—but tears of happiness now. "Oh, Jack—I think you'd be a fabulous councilor, the best Vancouver could possibly have! I don't know how I could have thought that you would...It's just been so stressful, what with Mother and your sister telling me I had to do this and that for our wedding, cramming in more and more guests—more *tofu*..."

Jack tipped her chin up. "Nobody is going to tell anybody anything, because *you* are going to marry *me*. Nobody else is going to be involved. No out-of-control wedding, no twentieth cousins twice-removed from Tuktoyaktuk."

"But—"

"As soon as we get back to Vancouver, Madge."

And there, in Union Station, he kissed her. For a lo-o-o-n-n-n-g time.

Talbot, Pantelli and I edged away. "That's some smooch," Pantelli observed. "Man, I could have finished the *Young Dendrologist's Encyclopedia* by now."

Talbot took me by the elbow and swung me round. "You better think about what happens when Madge and Jack, having turned sixty-five, finally end their smooch," he advised, not unkindly. "They may start pondering just how this LaFlamme mix-up happened."

Pantelli nodded, his eyes gleaming. "Yeah, Di. Bustin' into Jack's e-mail," he said and drew a finger across his throat.

But I wasn't feeling too worried. True, Madge and Jack

would be furious. They'd get over it, though. That was the thing about having loved ones. About belonging. You knew, no matter what, that they accepted you.

I checked on the smoochers. Note that I said I wasn't feeling *too* worried. Slightly concerned, yes.

They were still smooching. Phew! Off to one side, Toronto police officers were escorting Mrs. Chewbley off the train. In spite of being handcuffed, she nevertheless managed to transfer two chocolate creams from her pocket up to her mouth. Cheeks bulging, Mrs. Chewbley raised her hand-cuffed wrists and flapped her hands at me in a wave. And shrugged. So ends my chase for the king, the piano teacher seemed to be saying.

I can't say I liked Mrs. Chewbley, not with all the dangerous cups of tea she'd gone around plying people with. But at least, as a villain, she was a good sport.

I had a feeling her son wasn't going to be. Head Conductor Wiggins had heard from the police about Freddy. Two broken legs, a broken arm and a fractured hip, and Freddy had *still* been crawling into the cornfield after the envelope. In the prison ambulance, he'd fumed about "that little pipsqueak" and said some other words Mr. Wiggins refused to tell me.

I squinted. Past Mrs. Chewbley and the police, Ryan and his mom were heading out of the station. "Ryan!" I shouted—and paused. I wanted to yell something encouraging, but what? He had such challenges ahead of him that any of the usual messages—good on ya; all the best, huh?—I

could fling at him would sound silly. Besides, he was too
smart a kid for those.

Ryan couldn't tell where I was shouting from. He glanced
left, right and even up.

"End-of-smooch alert," Talbot advised.

Jack and Madge were marching toward me with quick-
ening steps. They kept glancing at each other, then at me,
and each time their faces grew more thunderous. I thought
I knew how Charles the Second had felt, waiting in that tree
for the Roundheads.

Then my mind went to a different king. All at once I had
an idea for what to tell Ryan.

"I'm going to make one of my trademark speedy exits,"
I informed Talbot and Pantelli.

"But I was looking forward to this," Pantelli objected.

Talbot laughed. "Don't crash into anything," he told
me.

I zoomed past the station's limestone columns to catch up
to Ryan and his mom. I had to keep looking up for Ryan's
mother because most of the people around me were taller
than I was. (Like, sigh, what else was new?)

"Oh, that girl's admiring the vaulted ceiling," a woman
remarked, riffling through her guidebook. "Soft gold tiles—so
majestic! Edward the Eighth officially opened it. 'You build
your stations like we build our cathedrals,' he remarked.
Such a witty king. Always knew the right thing to say...Ooo,
here's a photo of him. So handsome. So graceful."

Not that king, I thought. *Not that one.*

Distracted by the woman, I forgot Talbot's warning and collided with someone. The someone lost his footing momentarily, then bounced back.

"Beanstalk!" I exclaimed as the assistant head conductor curved over me in a disapproving *C*. "Sorry, I mean Assistant Head Conductor, er—"

"*Head* conductor is what you mean," Beanstalk smirked, straightening himself. "With Mr. Wiggins's abrupt retirement, I've been promoted. And though Gold-and-Blue policy is to value all passengers highly, I must say, Miss Galloway, that I am not sorry to see the last of you." He wagged a long finger at me. "One disturbance after another! I—"

"But we might see each other again," I said cheerfully. "Madge, Pantelli, Talbot and I are heading *back* to Vancouver by train too."

Beanstalk's forefinger flopped. His already naturally pale face blanched even more.

"Y'know," I mused, starting to walk away, "up to now I've always had problems with authority figures like you, Beanstalk. Maybe this time will be different. I'm going to make a real effort."

There was some sort of mangled cry behind me, but I couldn't pay attention to it. Ryan and his mom were leaving the station; Mrs. Zanatta was waving down a cab...

"Now what's so life-and-death, Dinah?" Mrs. Zanatta asked,

trying not to smile. "Or maybe I should say, what *isn't* life-and-death with you?"

We were at the curb outside the station, on Front Street West. Tall office buildings jutted up around us like asparagus spears, blotting out the sky. Cars stuck in jams honked. Masses of anxious-faced people wedged together in packs hurried by on the sidewalk. Toronto seemed at once grayer than Vancouver and more exciting.

Ryan was about to hurry on to the rest of his life too—and he had as much right to the feeling of belonging as I did, or anyone else.

His new doctor would help. But nothing would be easy. It never was, for anyone. Sometimes you got through the rough parts by singing and sometimes by just being too dang stubborn to give in to them. Or sometimes you didn't get through them and drank yourself silly and wrapped your car around a tree. And that was it. Kaput.

I had a story for Ryan that might make a difference to him. You never knew.

I sat down on the sidewalk. I was still wondering how to word what I had to say. It was occurring to me, for one thing, that Jonathan was wrong about shadows. You shouldn't try to banish the past, because it was part of you. My dad, his dying. Like it or not, I wouldn't be Dinah Galloway without those.

And I wouldn't want to be. When I sang, I was singing into the shadows as well as everywhere else. Maybe I'd tell Jonathan this one day.

But with Ryan I had to keep it simple.

Sing? Ryan mouthed.

"Not this time. Another time, though. Soon," I promised and laced my fingers through his. "Remember how Talbot told us that everyone was searching for a stamp? That on this stamp was a glamorous king, Edward the Eighth, who was smooth and clever?"

Ryan nodded.

"Right on. Well, Edward couldn't have cared too much about keeping his crown because he gave it up. And everyone was sorry. It was kind of like having a fun TV personality go into retirement."

I shoved my glasses up my nose, the better to gaze firmly through them at Ryan. This next part was the important one.

"So then Edward's younger brother George became king. George the Sixth. A lot of people thought George would be an embarrassment because he was shy and awkward, and," I paused for emphasis, "he stuttered."

Ryan's mouth formed a long O.

"Yup," I said. "A king who stuttered. And you know what? *He was the best king ever*. In spite of his stutter, he forced himself to give wonderful, inspiring speeches on the radio that got his country through the horrible Second World War. George the Sixth was courageous too. He and his family stayed on in London all the time the enemy was dropping bombs on the city. He refused to leave.

"Maybe George the Sixth wasn't smooth-talking," I finished. "But smooth doesn't count for a lot when things go wrong. It's what's here," I pounded my heart, "that's important."

Ryan's O was lake-sized now. "A st-stutterer?" he blurted. Then the O spread into a wide smile. He exclaimed, without stuttering at all, "That's Dinah-mite!"

Mrs. Zanatta was mopping at her eyes with a tissue. These grown-ups! To distract Ryan, our architect-in-the-making, from her silliness, I pointed up to the CN Tower. Even past these tall, spear-like buildings you could see it.

"Wow," Ryan said of the Tower, which stretched on and on, like the possibilities everyone should have.

Other books in the Dinah Galloway series

The Spy in the Alley
The Man in the Moonstone
The Mask on the Cruise Ship
The Summer of the Spotted Owl

Visit www.orcabook.com for more information on these books.